DETACHED

a novel by
LORENZO C. ROBERTSON

Tampa, Florida

An Ishai Book

Published by The Ishai Creative Group, Inc.
709 East Caracas Street • Tampa, Florida 33603-2328

Library of Congress Card Catalog No.: 98-941-96
ISBN # 1-892096-35-8
Copyright © 1999 by Lorenzo C. Robertson
All Rights Reserved

For Additional Information abour Ishai Books
Visit us on the web @ www.ishaibooks.com
or email us at Ishai Books @aol.com

Dedication

Detached is dedicated to my creator for without whom I will cease to exist.   To mothers, father, sister, brothers, sisters–in–law,brother–in–law, nieces, nephews and my partner I love you all.

Detached is dedicated to all those that endure the agony and pain of emotional detachment for reasons beyond their control. I hope that Detached will touch a part of your spirit and make your heart soar to emotional attachment.

Acknowledgements

First and foremost I would like to thank my creator for allowing me to be, for without His divine mercy I would cease to exist. Next I would like to thank my mothers and father for allowing me to just be me, for that I am truly grateful. I love you Maybell Robertson, L.C. Robertson and Allie M. Rollins.

To my sister and biggest critic, Sylvia, I love you for all your support and honesty you have always been my biggest fan and I have always tried to live up to the standards that you set for me.

To my brothers, Shaun, Antonio and Christopher, I love each of you and hope that in some small I have been or will be an inspiration to you to be better than you are today.

To my grandparents (Roosevelt & Eddie Lee Robertson, Perry Lee Robertson, Vienna Mae Robertson, Robert Lemuel Parrish, Clora Moore and Willie Moore) for their unwavering love and support over the years. To each of you thank you and I love you very much.

To a host of family and friends, thank you for your love and support, even when I didn't know you were giving it, thank you from the depths of my soul.

Thanks to my editor, Maggie Council and graphic artist, Elizabeth Flurkey.

Last, but certainly not least to my partner, Ricc, thank you for all your love, support and honesty. I Love you and hope that our life together will only get better, last longer and grow stronger as each day passes.

DETACHED

Wednesday, August 3, 1988

Today, Wednesday, August 3, 1988, was the first day of the rest of Jon's life. He was not doing what he needed to do with his life. Jon was not living life to his full potential, not sharing of himself with others and not making an effort to love himself or anyone else. Jon Knight was detached.

Reconstructing previous evenings was always difficult at first, but then something would trigger a memory, a person or a place from the night before. He prayed that tonight would be different, but he knew it would be more of the same.

Jon left the office in his black Mustang and went directly to happy hour at the Cactus Club, instead of going home first to change into his club clothes. He met a few friends out for drinks and left the bar to go home and change before heading to the Parliament House for dancing. The drive home was

1

uneventful. Unlike other times, today's drive home was not a nightmare; waking up lying across the bed with his clothes on not remembering how he got there. Today was different. Only two Tanqueray on the rocks with lime, and he did not feel the effects of the alcohol yet. Pulling his green Mustang into the parking space, Jon gathered his things from the back seat. Arms full of work stuff he could barely open the door to his apartment. Once inside, his arms spilled the work stuff onto the floor. He left the papers, folders and manuals on the floor.

Jon went into the bedroom and began to undress, tossing his shirt and tie on the bed, putting his belt on the belt rack and placing his pants in the dirty clothes hamper. He'd left his jacket in the living room with the other work stuff. Now, he began the task of looking for something to wear to the club. Gap jeans and a tight black T-shirt, he decided, and threw his club clothes across the bed.

In the kitchen Jon made himself a drink before he took his shower. Pouring himself a glass of Tanqueray over crushed ice with lime, he went to the bathroom. Adjusting the water temperature until it was just right, he took a swig of the cocktail before placing the glass on the counter. Jon got in the shower to prepare for his night of decadence. He always liked to keep the private areas fresh because you never knew.

As the hot pulsating water pounded his body, he began his routine. The water felt like a passionate lover brutally massaging his back and it felt good. Standing there, he let the water wash over him. The fiery water washed over his body like waves crashing against the shore of the ocean during a hurricane. Jon invariably enjoyed taking hot sensual showers, alone. Steaming water cascaded over Jon's body as he stood there savoring each drop. Jon explored his body like a lover, caressing and touching himself as thewater engulfed him. He grabbed his soap and began to lather his body. His body covered with white foam from his neck to his toes. He took great care enjoying his showers because he knew it was only time and place where he had solitude.

Getting out of the shower Jon reached for his towel and began to dry his 6' 1" honey-dipped muscular body. Dripping with water, he walked across the room. Putting the Eurythmics's CD, *Be Yourself Tonight*, he programmed *Would I Lie to You* and *There Must be an Angel (Playing with my Heart)* to repeat as he continued to dry his body and danced around the room. As, Annie Lennox blared from the speakers, Jon washed his face and admired his reflection in the steam streaked mirror. He finished getting ready and was preparing to get out of the house before 10:00 p.m. Just as he was about to walk out the door, the phone rang. He decided not to answer it. Standing at the door, he listened to the message.

"Yo', Jon this is Eric just checking in to see what was up tonight?" he paused. "I got that package for you, so call me tonight," he hung up the phone. Jon decided that he would deal with Eric tomorrow and not entertain him or the package until then. Walking out the door Jon headed for the Parliament House or PH as the club kids called it, to do a little dancing and drinking. He arrived and looked for a parking space that was close and pulled into the grass space. Looking in the rear view mirror, he checked to make sure he looked good for the children. Brushing his hand across his hair, he was off to a night of deviation.

Inside the Parliament House the music pounded his eardrums. The smoke burned his eyes. Looking around the disco, he spotted his best friend Cyril standing at the bar on the other side of the disco. Jon quickly walked over to him.

"Hey, bitch how the hell are you?" Jon said as he grabbed and hugged Cyril.

"I'm fine, slut! Can't you tell? Why are you here so early? You don't usually make an appearance until one or two in the morning? Oh, you're on the prowl tonight. What you got a taste for tonight?" Cyril said.

"I just left Cactus not too long ago and thought that I might

3

make it an early night. You know I do need my beauty rest. I need a cocktail," Jon said doing his best Eartha Kitt .

Jon leaned over the bar and ordered a Tanqueray on the rocks with lime and a Captain Morgan and Coke for Cyril. To get a better view of the boys dancing, he turned around. The bartender tapped Jon on the shoulder to get his attention. Jon paid the bartender and took the drinks over to Cyril sitting at a high bar table.

"Here's your cocktail."

"Thanks, honey. I'll get the next round. Okay, baby."

Looking over the boys on the floor to see if there was anything of interest to him, Jon quickly dismissed 80 percent of the bar because they were the regulars. Jon sat and scrutinized the dancing boys until he saw something that looked quite appetizing. In the middle of the same old folks, danced a cute little Puerto Rican boy. He looked between about twenty and twenty-five years old. The Puerto Rican boy danced in a little white crochet tank top baring defined abs and shorts that accented his hot little butt and muscular legs. Jon sat there, transfixed on this gorgeous 5'10" boy, with dark curly hair. Looking at Jon, Cyril knew that he had seen the seductive Latin boy dancing. Cyril decided, as he always did, that the Puerto Rican boy would be called Latin Prey, until they found out his real name.

Cyril began to sing, "I'm gonna get you, baby. I'm gonna get you, yes I am."

Cyril always told Jon that "I'm gonna get you" was his theme song and Jon usually got what or whom he wanted. The men dancing all looked at Latin Prey in his crocheted outfit. Men began swarming around the kid, like vultures after their prey. He was quite a specimen, but Jon opted to look and not fall into the mad rush to entice the young one for his carnal pleasures, at least not tonight.

Jon caught Latin Prey's eye. He acknowledged Jon's tease and responded with a quick wink and an air kiss. Jon and Latin Prey flirted the rest of the night, on the dance floor, at the bar, in the show room, all over the disco, but neither spoke a word to the other, which was unusual for Jon.

Cyril and Jon continued to keep the waiters and bartenders engaged. The waiter, a cute little blond blue eyed boy with no shirt and the body of life, looked at Jon and Cyril for the Tanqueray on the rocks with lime and Captain Morgan's and Coke signal. In unison, Jon and Cyril, waved their hands in the air. Their bodies wavered from already too much consumption of alcohol.

Looking around the room for Latin Prey Jon sat reeling on the stool as the music pumped; the men and women danced. Latin Prey caught Jon's eye as he left the disco. He blew a kiss to Jon and vanished out the door, into the night. Jon jumped from his bar stool to catch Latin Prey. Jon couldn't make it through the crowd quick enough. By the time Jon made his way to the door the boy was gone and so was any chance of Jon having the Latin kid tonight.

"Damn!" Jon screamed as he stood outside the PH.

Jon stood in the alcove looking for the hot Latin man. Speeding by the entrance of the Parliament House, Latin Prey zipped pass blowing Jon another kiss and waving bye-bye. In utter disbelief Jon stood there for a moment thinking that he would get him; just wait until they meet. Pushing people aside as he trudged through the crowd, Jon went back to his bar stool where Cyril waited for the Latin Prey report. Jon waved to the waiter to bring another round of cocktails although the ones on the table were not finished. Gulping down his gin, Jon told Cyril that Latin Prey was gone and he did not get a chance to meet him. Looking around for the waiter Jon sat there impatiently waiting on another drink, which he did not need. Cyril spotted Bruce, a piece that he'd been fucking and called him over.

"What's up, baby? It's been a while since I've seen that cute smile of yours. Where have you been hiding?" Bruce uttered with a slight Jamaican accent.

"Trying to contain myself until I found you again. I know that the Misses won't let you out too often. So I bide my time until thenext time you are allowed out of the house to play," Cyril spoke softly into Bruce's ear.

"Hello. My name is Jon, Jon said as he extended his hand.

"Leave it to these two and you might be standing there for quite some time waiting on an introduction,"

"Ernest, very nice to meet you,"

Ernest pulled up a stool and joined Jon and Cyril at the table. Bruce stood between Cyril's legs, arms around his neck kissing and nibbling his ears. Jon and Ernest began talking. Drinks were forth coming for the eighth or tenth round. Neither Jon or Cyril could remember the number they were up to at this point. The tipsy clique raised their glasses high in the air, clinking. They laughed and cheered for no apparent reason, besides the fact that they were intoxicated.

Ernest invited everyone back to his house for a nightcap and swimming. Cyril and Jon told the guys that before they left they needed to say a few goodbyes. Jon and Cyril dismissed themselves to discuss the plans for the night. Jon told Cyril that he wasn't really impressed with Ernest, but since Latin Prey had gone for the evening he thought what the hell. They laughed and returned to Bruce and Ernest. The motley crew was on their way, more alcohol.

The clan converged on Ernest's beautiful home in Winter Park. They entered the living room and Ernest flipped on the lights. He told everyone to make themselves at home. Jon made his way to the love seat and plopped down. The cutesy couple made their way to the sofa. Bruce sat on the sofa. Cyril sat as close as they could possibly get without sitting in his lap. Ernest made drinks for the foursome. He was a very good bartender; heavy on the alcohol, light on the chaser. Bringing the drinks to Bruce and Cyril, Ernest asked Jon to assist with their drinks and he obliged. Jon decided to make a toast.

"May our bonds of gin, scotch and rum hold us together 'til

tomorrow comes. Cheers! Drink up everybody!" Jon slurred enthusiastically. Jon drank his concoction in one swig and went to the bar to make another. Jon felt he was on the verge of doing something he would regret, but he never regretted anything he did, he just took everything in stride. Standing behind the bar, he took a big gulp of his next drink and walked across the room. Joining the party, Jon sat on the love seat next to Ernest. Cyril and Bruce were in their own world and oblivious to their surroundings. Ernest and Jon tried to have stimulating conversation concerning the Stealth Bomber, origin of man and other topics that their inebriated state would not allow to transpire. As, Jon had predicted tonight ended, like many nights before. More alcohol. More sex.

Thursday, August 4, 1988

J on wiped the sleep from his eyes, he realized he was not in his own bed. He began to look around the bedroom to see if anything looked familiar to help him figure out where he was and who he slept with last night. Morning had come and once again he was in the bed of a stranger. Already an hour late Jon needed to get home and then to work. His body reeked of gin. He smelled himself and the pungent odor stung his nostrils. Today was yet another day working through a hangover fog. He looked around the room to find his jeans, because last night was one of those let-it-all-hang out nights, no underwear. Walking barefoot around the room Jon spied his black T-shirt quickly put it on.

Now for the decisive moment, whose house was this? Did he really want to know? Standing there dumbfounded Jon racked his brain for an identifying clue. There were none. The decor of the bedroom gave no hint as the owner of the bedroom. Still, he stood there looking at the tumbled black and white sheets on the bed and the used condoms on the floor. His only comfort, *at least we were safe.*

Making his way across the room, he stood in front of the dresser and looked at the staring face in the mirror. Face swollen from alcohol and lack of sleep. Bloodshot eyes with saddle bags. Luckily, as the day progressed, the puffiness under his eyes would smooth out and he would have that hand-some face he had grown accustomed to. He stood there and tried to remember the night before.

The door to the bedroom opened and Jon stared in the face of someone that he didn't know. He looked at Jon and said good morning. Jon looked blankly and returned the greeting. He sensed that Jon didn't remember his name. He gave Jon that, *I don't believe this bastard*, look.

"My name is Ernest in case you forgot?" Ernest said sorrowful-ly that Jon didn't remember his name.

"I'm sorry, but I am terrible with names and I had few too many cocktails last night so my memory is a little fuzzy. Do you think I can take a quick shower?" Jon spoke groggily through his thick alcohol coated tongue.

"Not a problem," Ernest said as he walked to the closet to get Jon a towel and face cloth. Taking the towel and face cloth Jon walked into the bathroom closing the door behind him. The room was a pale grey with white and grey border. The long granite counter was clear and empty of the usual tooth paste, combs, brushes and other bathroom amenities. Jon leaned against the sink thinking about where he was and how he had gotten there. He looked in the mirror for answers that were not there. He began to undress, which didn't take much, since he only had on two pieces of clothing, T-shirt and jeans.

Folding his clothes and placing them on the counter, he stood there naked looking again in the mirror for answers. He stood there as the tears streamed down his face. How did his life get so fucked up? Waking up in the bed of strangers checking the room to make sure condoms were used. This is no way to live and he needed to make a change. Famous last words; this was the same chanted mantra he had spouted for as long as he could remember. Why would this time be any different? For the next few days he would act differently, but then he would fall back into the same routine. Today was only Wednesday and Friday, party night, was rapidly approaching and that always meant partying with friends new and old.

What would make this revelation and promise different from all the rest? Tears streaming down his face Jon sat there hoping that some inner voice would speak and make everything all right. No voice spoke. For what seemed an eternity Jon sat there before getting into the shower. He quickly showered. Jon stood in the middle of the bathroom putting his clothes on. The knock on the door interrupted Jon's thoughts about his fucked up life.

"Wanna cup of java?" Ernest asked from behind the closed door.

"Thanks, but I've got to be going? Gotta get to work."

"I can make it to go, I have one of those coffee cups with the wide bottom that sits on the dashboard of your car. I can get it for you if you 'd like," Ernest said hurriedly.

"Thanks, that will be fine."

"How do you take your coffee black with a little sugar, like your men?"

"That's right. However did you know?" Jon teased.

"I just took a wild guess. Let me go. It will be ready when you come out of the bathroom," Ernest said before he rushed to the kitchen to prepare Jon's coffee.

Jon leaned against the counter and questioned himself about his life and the direction that it had taken over the past few years. His job was going well. He had a good circle of friends. Family was supportive. Why did he have the need to be so self–destructive? This question plagued Jon.

Making his way to the kitchen Jon was in a hurry to get the coffee and get out. Jon lied to Ernest that he would give him a call and that they would get together for dinner a movie or something. He gave him a quick peck on the cheek and was out of the house in a flash.

In his car Jon quickly cranked up and was on his way home. Driving through town during the early morning hours the streets were clear because everybody else was at work, already. Jon put the windows down in the car to let the fresh morning air help with the morning hangover. He pulled his trusty eye drops out of the center compartment and dropped a few in both eyes. This was the way he tried to get rid of the bloodshot hangover peepers. He stuck his head out the window to let the fresh misty air blow over his face. Zipping along at a rapid pace, he made his way across town in record time.

Pulling into his parking space he jumped out of the car and ran inside to get dressed for work. Starched Kenneth Gordon white shirt, Canali grey two-button suit and a platinum silk tie would be the attire for the day. Luckily, he had just picked up his clothes from the cleaners Monday. Racing into his apart-ment he made his way to the bedroom and dressed for the office, hurriedly. Jon sprayed Sybaris on his wrists and neck, spoke with his assistant to reschedule his two morning appoint-ments as early as possible. She told him that his early appoint-ment would not reschedule and she chose to wait until he came into the office. Jon asked to speak with Ms. Jones and he explained to her that he would not be available to meet with her today. His schedule was full today and he apologized for not making it to the office for her appointment. Ms. Jones was not pleased with this situation but she let him off the hook, this time.

Completing his preparation for work, Jon slipped on his black leather Sam & Libby shoes. Tossing some multivitamin in his mouth, grabbing office files, papers and manuals Jon made a mad dash back to his car and was on the road to the office in less than ten minutes.

Jon walked in the office two hours late, two missed appointments. The office busybody, Mildred, was in the reception area when he arrived. She glanced at her watch and gave Jon a *thanks for joining us*, look. He ignored her and went straight to his office closing the door behind him. His assistant Claire, sat at her desk. She was dark woman with afrocentric features. She stood about 5' 4" tall and her hair cut in a pageboy. She buzzed him to check if he needed anything other than the files for his next two appointments, which she had placed on his desk. There was nothing else he needed. The two sessions were uneventful; just more of the same. All the clients needed someone to listen to them bitch, moan and vent. Jon labored through the remainder of the day doing his best to keep his hangover at bay.

At five o'clock the day had finally finished. Jon was in his car and on his way home by five o' five. This was normal, Jon rarely stayed in the office past five o 'clock. Today was no exception. He needed to get home and get some rest. Driving along he could feel his body. He could feel the blood coursing through his veins, his skin shed, he could feel the hair growing on his head and he needed to be home in bed, now. Eyes closed cruising along the interstate at a harrowing pace. Jon careened. Narrowly missing a truck, Jon's peepers popped open; he swerved to avoid the concrete median. Slowing his pace Jon reached into the center compartment to find his eye drops. He dropped a few in each sliver. The liquid burned, then soothed his eyes. This would refresh him until he made it home. Turning the volume up to a pounding pulsating deafening clamor, Jon listened to LLCool J's, *I'm going back to Cali* the rest of the trip home. Pulling into his space, Jon gathered his briefcase and jacket and made his way to his apartment door. Once inside he dropped everything on his desk , made his way to the bedroom and fell across the bed in the bedroom.

The phone rang ,and it was Eric. Jon rolled across the bed to catch the phone before the answering machine picked up. They talked briefly. Eric needed to deliver the package so Jon told Eric to come on over. Sitting up in the bed Jon looked at the clock and realized it was ten o' clock. He was still in his work clothes.

Feeling refreshed from his rather long nap Jon undressed and jumped in the shower.   After his shower, he put on some shorts and a tank. Listening to Diana Ross', *Red, Hot Rhythm & Blue* album, Jon made himself a cocktail and waited for Eric.

 His desk was cluttered with work that he wouldn't get to tonight. At the office he would complete the client analysis and report due tomorrow by the end of the day.   Not allowing himself to think about anything Jon danced around the living room gyrating to the pounding music.   Lost in the music Jon was brought back to the present when he heard the sound of the door knocker. He went over to the door and peeked to see who was there, hoping it was Eric. The peep hole was dark so Jon could not see who was there. He opened the door anyway.

Eric, medium height and build, stood there waiting to enter. Stepping aside Jon allowed Eric into the living room. They greeted each other, with a manly handshake and embrace, the sort that athletes do on televised award shows. Jon offered Eric a seat and asked if he wanted a drink? Eric said that he'd make it and told Jon to get his stuff.   Jon retrieved a small plate from the cupboard. A short straw and shiny razor blade sat on the plate. Wiping the white powder residue from the plate, Jon licked his finger.

They sat in the living room, drinking. Eric pulled out a small triangular plastic container filled with a white powder substance. Shaking the bag to check the quantity, Eric passed the open container to Jon. He stuck his finger in putting some white powder on the tip of his tongue rubbing the rest across his teeth. He dumped the contents on the small plate. Using the blade, he began to sift and chop the white powder. Moving the blade back and forth across the mound making sure to smooth out any clusters, Jon's movements were like a surgeon's.

Jon arranged the white powder into four thick lines leaving the excess in a pile. Kneeling by the coffee table, Jon put the straw to his right nostril holding his other nostril closed. Bending over to the small plate, Jon inhaled the first line on the plate and reeled back. Sliding the plate across the table Jon passed Eric the straw and he repeated Jon's act. Eric slid the plate back to Jon. Jon took the straw and began to sniff one of the remaining two lines of cocaine. Eric indicated that he did not want another hit, so Jon consumed the last line on the plate.

Pushing the plate back to Eric, Jon went to the sink to put some water up his nose from his middle finger. Eric cut the rest of the cocaine into more thick lines and snorted one up immediately. Not asking if Eric wanted another drink, Jon made more drinks and brought them to the table.

Taking the straw Jon whiffed up two lines and pushed the plate over to Eric, he did the last line wiping the remnants rubbing his finger across his gums. Eric asked Jon for an assessment of the cocaine. He indicated that it was great and wanted to buy a couple of grams. Eric pulled a larger container from his pocket passing it to Jon.

He opened the container and poked in a finger and rubbed the coke across his gums. The quality seemed to be the same as what he'd sampled. He gave Eric the money and they sat there for a while. Jon grabbed a tissue to wipe his nose draining from the coke. Eric and Jon were ready for a night out. They had one last cocktail before hitting the streets. Eric decided he needed to make a few more rounds to other friends, customers. he told jon that he would meet him later at the club.

Walking into the Parliament House Jon looked on the dance floor and there he was, Latin Prey. He was dancing alone. Jon caught Latin Prey's eye. Jon motioned for him to come over. He did.

"I remember you from last night. My name is Jon," he said

extending his hand.

"My name is Juan. Why didn't you say something to me last night? I thought you were very attractive and wanted to meet you. But I don't make a habit of walking up to total strangers to say hello," he said with a slight Puerto Rican accent.

"Well, last night you seemed to have the whole club trying to meet you, so I just thought that if is meant to be then it will be!"

"So, I guess it was meant to be, here we are together talking and . . ."

"Looking good," Jon said in a too fake Puerto Rican accent.

They laughed at his attempt at a Puerto Rican accent. Juan took Jon by the hand pulling him out on the dance floor. They danced. The night was young. Drinks. Jon laughed and danced the night away with Juan. Drinks. The evening was shaping into one of seduction. The strange part was Jon couldn't detect if he were seducing Juan or vice versa. Either way the evening was going great.

At the end of the night Jon asked Juan what was he doing after the club closed. He told Jon that he would probably go back to the hotel. Jon asked if wanted to come over to his place for a nightcap, before going to the hotel with sister, brother in-law and kids. Juan agreed and followed Jon to his place.

Jon arrinving at home, remembered Eric never showed up at the club, which was not usual for him, but Jon had more pressing business at hand... *Juan*. Once home and settled, Jon asked if there was any particular type of music he wanted to listen, to. Juan suggested anything by Anita Baker would suffice. Glancing through his CD's, Jon found Anita's *Rapture*. He put it in and programmed the repeat mode. He lit some candles, turned off the lights and slid next to Juan on the sofa. Jon looked deep into Juan's soft brown eyes, playfully running his finger through his hair. Putting his arm around him, Juan nuzzled into Jon's chest. He placed his arm around Jon's abdomen. Looking up at Jon, he looked away.

"What's the matter?" Jon asked in a hushed tone.

"I'm just looking at how handsome you are. Then I wonder why are you with me?" Juan said shyly.

"Because you're gorgeous! You are one of the most attractive, sexy, alluring men I have met in quite some time. And I can't wait to see you out of those clothes," Jon said with a sexy undertone.

"Oh, you want to see me out of my clothes. Is that why you brought me back to your place? Well, I never!" Juan said in mock indignation.

"That was part of the plan. I didn't think you would have a problem with that?" Jon said as he moved in to gently kiss Juan's waiting lips.

Kissing softly Jon allowed his lips to open slightly to feel the warmth of Juan's mouth. Juan responded. As they kissed, they began to let their hands explore the other's body. Holding on for dear life Juan could not believe the burning desire that erupted through his body when Jon's mouth moved to his neck. Tossing his head back to enjoy the moment Juan realized that Jon was taking him to pleasure points he hadn't experienced before. Jon undressed Juan. Juan lay there bare. Lying there contemplating the next surge of desire Juan braced himself for what was to come next. Jon told Juan to stay there. He needed to get some oil. Returning with the baby oil Jon took Juan's feet and massaged each thoroughly. Jon gently rolled Juan onto his stomach. Massaging each calf Jon leaned over and kissed the back of his knees. Juan squirmed with delight. Kneading his thighs Jon moved his hands to Juan's little round firm butt and began to massage, giving each cheek equal treatment. Rubbing the small of his back Jon added a little pressure; Juan raised with excitement. Jon reached for more oil. Sliding his fingers up and down his spine Juan could not take the pleasure; he let out a sigh. Sighing indicated Jon hit the right spots, so he continued. Massaging his body, Jon moved from the shoulders and then to the neck. Juan's body was totally relaxed and ready for the next wave of passion that was sure to come.

Jon picked Juan up and carried him to the bedroom. The room smelled of scented candles. Beside the bed was a wine cooler with a bottle of wine and two glasses. Anita Baker's music drifted into the room like waves on the shore of a lake. Juan lay there looking at Jon as he slowly seductively took off his clothes. He dropped his clothes on the floor and got into bed. Jon pulled Juan to him and kissed him passionately and Juan kissed him back. Jon gave Juan a glass of wine.

"May we make love until the morning comes and that the morning never comes," Jon said as he continued kissing Juan tasting the sweetness of the wine.

Jon looked into Juan eyes to see if everything was all right and his eyes said that all was well with the world. Jon slowly tantalized Juan moving on top of him kissing him from head to toe. Jon left no spot on Juan's body untouched by his sensuous lips. Juan lay there entranced by Jon's gentle love making. He put his hand behind Juan's neck held and kissed him deeply. He was enchanted with the nectar of Juan's mouth. Juan clung to Jon like a python wrapped around its prey. Bodies entwined. They made love. More alcohol. More sex.

Friday, August 5, 1988

The early morning sun pierced through the window blinds awakening Jon from his slumber. Juan was still in his arms. He laid there for a moment and collected his thoughts. Last night, love making was wonderful, Jon thought. If Juan didn't live in New York, he would be the perfect lover for him. Jon got up trying not to disturb Juan's siesta.

Jon looked at the clock and realized that he had time before he got ready for work to make a little breakfast for him and his lover. In the kitchen Jon made coffee, eggs and toast. He went back in the bedroom and gently nudged Juan. He awakened staring up at Jon. Standing there in his silk black and white polka dot robe he leaned over and kissed Juan softly on the lips.

"I made breakfast," Jon whispered to Juan.

"The only breakfast I want is standing right there. Come on

back to bed. I need to feel you again. You've touched that spot in me that no one has ever found. So, will you come back and touch that spot again and again? " Juan said with a sly smileover his slight Puerto Rican accent.

"I'd love to but I don't have time to love you the way I want and I don't ever want to rush loving you. So, if you can wait until tonight I will do my damnedest to satisfy your every want, need and desire," Jon whispered into his ear.

Juan pulled Jon into bed. Passions erupted. They made love. Not rushed but at a quicker pace than the night before. They laid there spent dripping with sweat from the early morning love making. Jon vowed that he would still make it to work on time. He jumped up and made it to the shower. As he stood in the shower water hitting his chest, he felt a hand touch his back. Juan had joined him in the shower. They washed each other. They laughed and played in the water. Jon rinsed the soap suds from his body and got out of the shower.

Jon was dressed in the kitchen having a cup of coffee when Juan finally emerged from the bedroom. Juan was dressed in jeans and a Hard-Rock cafe T-shirt. Not the clothes he had on the night before. He informed Jon that he always carried extra stuff in his back pack for those occasions when he didn't make it home. This was not a practice he made a habit, but he liked to be prepared, Boy Scout training and all. Looking at the way those jeans fit his hot little body turned Jon immediately on and now he wanted to repeat the earlier performance. Time did not permit.

They hugged and shared one final kiss. Juan was out the door he needed to catch up with his sister to let her know that he was still alive. They made plans for that evening.

Looking for his little plate Jon rubbed his finger across the plate then over his gums. Taking the plastic container from the plate, he emptied a small amount onto the plate. Using the blade he sifted and designed two fat lines on the plate. Straw up nostril, sniffing. One line. Then the other. Over to the sink for a little water, plate back in the cupboard and Jon was out the door on his way to work.

The office was especially busy everyone was preparing their client analysis and client reports for the afternoon deadline. Claire was not at her desk or in his office. He needed her now; they had a lot of work to tackle today and he did not have time for her to be out of place. Putting his briefcase and other papers on his desk, he paged Claire to report immediately to his office. She arrived almost before he'd finished the announcement. He directed her to a stack of files and requested that she sort and file them before starting on the reviews and the client analysis, not to mention his revised client report. Claire looked over-whelmed at the amount of work expected of her today. She just took it all in stride and dug in to get the reports completed.

"Claire, I need you to order lunch in today. There is a spe-cial project that I need your assistance with before the analysis report can be completed," Jon said sternly.

"Chinese, is that okay with you?"

"Chinese is fine. Now, let's get this special project finished so we can make deadline on the other reports and analysis. I need the files on Ms. Jones, Mr. Johnson, and Mr. and Mrs. Sampson," Jon spoke in a rushed direct voice.

"Those three files are on your desk. I thought those would be the ones used for the analysis.I put the Onyx Group files on your desk, also. The case studies there might be of assistance with the client reports," she said matter-of-factly.

Claire was always on top of everything that Jon needed; sometimes even the things he didn't need. Working together in the office for about three years, Jon and Claire had a chemistry that worked like a well-oiled machine. They clicked from day one. A single mother of two, Claire was a great mother. She expected and got only the best from her two children. Jon and Claire never had a cross word. Not that Jon did not push her to the breaking point sometimes, but she always remained cool as a cucumber. She covered for him on many occasions when he would come late or just not show up until after lunch. They had a great working relationship and Jon knew he had the best assistant in the office.

By the end of the day all the reports and analysis were completed and in the vice-president's office ready for review. Jon and Claire were exhausted from the breakneck speed of the day. They sat in Jon's office and collected their energy. To show his gratitude, Jon gave Claire Monday off. The reports would not have been completed without her tenacity. Putting the files and old reports away Claire came across a referral new client analysis file that was not completed and put it in Jon's to be filed tray. He did not want to do any more work today so he didn't even look at the file. Jon told Claire he would finish tidying his office and for her to go home. Jon sat there feeling quite good about himself hecompleted his projects and still had about an hour before the deadline. All in all it had been a great day. He talked himself into going to happy hour. He left the office and headed for the nearest bar.

Jon ordered another Tanqueray on the rocks with lime, the barkeep knew his order by the third cocktail in an hour. Eating Chex-Mix, Jon sat there telling this guy about his fantastic day. The guy really could care less, but that did not deter Jon. He just kept on talking and talking about work. About six o 'clock Jon decided to leave the bar go home and get ready to meet Juan. Leaving the bar Jon made it to his car and began his trek home. Jon made it home.

Juan was there waiting when Jon got home. Looking as cute as ever in fitted black pants and a tight black shirt that looked to be painted on his small muscular body. Black leather belt with a huge silver buckle. Hestood there sexy as hell, hair slicked back curly and glossy. Jon was pleased to see Juan. He walked to his door. Holding Juan for what seemed an eternity. They made their way into the apartment. Jon went directly to the bedroom to take off the work day. Looking for some glasses to make a few cocktails Juan discovered the small plate and its contents. Juan began to make drinks. He put the small plate on the counter. Taking the drinks to the bedroom Juan did not mention   the   small   plate.

"I know that I don't know you. I'll be back in New York on Sunday, but why didn't you hook me up with a little taste," Juan said with his slight Puerto Rican accent looking hungrily at Jon.

"What are you talking about?"

"Yo', man how 'bout just a little a hit?"

"Oh, Juan, would you like a little blow?"

The small plate was on the counter. Looking at Juan, Jon tried to remember whether he'd left the plate out or what. Juan shook his head to suggest that he put the plate on the counter. Moving the plate to the coke table Jon and Juan sat across from each other. Pouring a generous amount of coke onto the plate Jon used the same blade to chop, sift and make four lines for himself and his lover. Being a gracious host Jon offered the plate to Juan first. He accepted kneeling to draw the coke into his nose. He repeated the act and stood breathing deeply to draw all the coke into his brain. Taking the straw from Juan's hand Jon quickly sniffed up the remaining two lines holding one nose hole closed to achieve the maximum effect of the cocaine. More coke. More cocktails. More coke. More cocktails.

Coke and alcohol combined for a night of unimaginable pleasure. The lovers began with a torrid kiss. Savagely tearing away at Juan's clothes Jon began to caress his naked body. Not allowing Jon to have all the enjoyment, Juan ripped Jon's shirt and began to recklessly suck on Jon's nipples. Pulling Jon's pants down to exposed his manhood Juan swallowed him completely. Reaching for the small container on the coke table Juan sprinkled the white powder onto Jon's raging erection. He swallowed him again and again. Jon could not take the primal sexual stirring hewas experiencing. This was the first time his penis felt this amazing sensation. He had never put coke on his dick before. This was a new episode. Jon savored the palpitation of his member. More coke. More cocktails. Juan relished each touch of Jon's lips on his body. Juan was lying on the sofa naked. Jon stepped out of his shorts and lay onto top of Juan. Their bodies meshed. They made love. They had raw uninhibited sex. Juan's spot was touched over and over. Passion bathed over their sex. Sex was immaculate. Hours later the sex was still immaculate. Enervated, Juan lay with his head on Jon's chest. Jon rested with his eyes closed ,exhausted.

Around midnight Jon woke up and was ready to party. It was Friday, the start of the weekend. Getting up from between the coke table and the sofa, Jon felt his paramour's body pressed tightly to his own. He brushed Juan's hair and kissed his cheek. Jon tried to awaken Juan, gently. His soft brown eyes opened slightly. Looking at Jon he inquired about the time. Feeling all the passion swirling through his body, Juan needed to be held. Just to meld into Jon's body once again. Embracing him, Juan clung to Jon.

In a rest room stall at the PH Jon bumped a few spots of coke using the coke depository between his thumb and finger. He sprinkled more coke for Juan. He sniffed. Licking the coke residue Jon pushed open the door and they headed to the dance floor. The disco was crowded. The lovers got a great deal of attention as they walked hand in hand throuhg the disco floor. Maneuvering Juan to a high bar table, they sat and looked over the crowd. Jon didn't need to take a lap before committing to a spot. He had found someone already. Blondie's heart of Glass pumped throughout the club.

Cyril spotted Jon and ran over to ask about Ernest when he saw Latin Prey. He just walked up and sang Jon's theme song. They both laughed while Juan sat there oblivious to the joke. Cyril introduced himself in his, oh-so-forward way and explained the joke to Juan. The trio laughed. Jon told Cyril that Juan was leaving on Sunday going back to New York, but they had made plans to spend time together before his departure

and when he
visited New York in a month or so.

"Where is Bruce?" Jon asked looking around Cyril like he was hiding Bruce in his pocket.

"Oh, you know that bitch won't let him out but a few times a month, so we have to make the best of it whenever we can. He will try to get away over the weekend and we will spend some time at my place, I pray. Don't give me that stare," Cyril said, looking a little lonely.

"I'm not going to say a word. If I have told you once I have told you a thousand times get that married man out of your life. Find someone who is, first of all, gay. Second of all, single, and not one of those see-you-when-I-can-see-you men. But I won't say a word!" Jon spoke sternly and decisively.

"I thought you weren't gonna give me a lecture 'bout this? Jon, this is my life and I know what I'm doing. I am not hung up on Bruce. He gets out of the house a few times a month we get together and that's that. I don't want nothing else from him. Just hot sex and no commitment, no relationship. I like it when I like it, but don't tie me down."

"I just worry about you. I love you. You're like my brother and I just want the best for you. I don't care what you say and how hard you try to convince me otherwise I know that Bruce means more to you than a roll in the hay. Albeit, a hot roll in the hay. We've have this discussion before so I will just shut up. Cocktails, anyone?" Jon asked transcending from serious ending in a jovial tone.

"You are wrong my brother, Bruce is just a fuck. No more no less. Captain Morgan and coke. Thank you very much," Cyril said.

"If the sex is hot and nobody's hurt. I don't see what the problem is?" Juan asked, looking at Jon.

"I've been down this road with Cyril too many times. Calls all times of the night. Worried 'bout why didn't so and so call. Why doesn't he want me the way that I want him? It always starts out were just fucking. But every time Cyril falls in love and is left alone. Then we are on the phone or together. Him crying. Me consoling. I just don't want him to go through this bullshit again. But, he never listens. So I can't help, but luv'im and be there for him," Jon said glancing between Juan and Cyril.

"I understand my best friend's the same way. Always looking for Mr. Right, but he can't be gay. That is always a problem," Juan stated understandably.

"God damn it, you two are cut from the same fucking cloth. Let's talk 'bout something, else. Please!!!" exclaimed Cyril.

They both looked at each other. Cyril stood there feeling dejected because deep down inside at his core he knew they were both correct. He wanted Bruce and was on the verge of falling in love with yet another married man. He didn't really know how to break away from Bruce, so he would continue to see him, knowing that he would get hurt in the end, as usual.

Placing the libations on the bar table, the waiter stood there waiting impatiently for Jon to pay for the drinks. They took their drinks, clinked the glasses in the air and took long swallows. Putting the Tanqueray on the rocks with lime on the table Jon leaned over the table and kissed Juan on the cheek. Cyril just looked at the two of them and made his way across the room.

"Cyril! Cyril!" Jon yelled, but Cyril was out of ear shot.

Pulling his stool closer to Juan they sat there absorbing the ambience of the club people and the night. Sitting there together, the coke was wearing thin and they both needed another bump. Tapping his nose indicating another hit, Jon motioned for Juan to follow. They quickly drank their liquor concoctions and made their way to the rest room. In the stall Jon used the corner of a matchbook cover to penetrate the white powdery substance in the plastic bag. Placing the contents under Juan's nose Jon held the matchbook as steady as he could, wavering from the alcohol in his system. Snorting the powder up his nose Juan held his head back and breathed heavily, flushing the toilet to drown out his noise. Poking into the bag again Jon held the substance under his nose this time and sniffed. He held his nostril inhaling the cocaine into his head. They stood there as the water finished circling the toilet bowl. Jon wiped the corner of the matchbook cover and rubbed the finger across his gums. Placing the bag and matchbook in his pocket Jon pulled Juan to him. They kissed. Noise. They wandered back into the back to he disco and found a table.

The whirling lights from the disco ball and light show beckoned Jon to the dance floor. He grabbed Juan's had to trip the light fantastic. On the floor they gyrated to Vanity 6's *Nasty Girl*. The music pounded their eardrums and vibrated through their bodies. Cyril was on the floor getting freaky with some guy. The guy held Cyril tightly as they moved across the dance floor. Jon pulled Juan so that they could be near Cyril and his dancer friend. The DJ mixed Prince and Sheila E's seductive *Erotic City* over *Nasty Girl*. They danced until they were winded.

Juan, drenched with sweat, pulled Jon close to him and indicated that he needed a drink. Wiping his face with his hand, Jon left the dance floor. Standing at the bar, Jon got Cyril's attention and gestured to find out if he wanted a drink. Enthusiastically Cyril motioned yes. Leaning over the bar Jon ordered drinks and turned to see the children dance, holding Juan next to him. Picking up their glasses from the bar they walked over to an empty table, with Cyril not too far behind. He'd lost his dancer in the crowd. Cyril grabbed his rum and coke, taking a huge gulp. He stood there panting from the dance floor exercise. They sat. More alcohol. More coke. More alcohol. More coke.

Closing time at the Parliament House Juan and Jon swayed to the front door, Jon said his goodbyes, hugging and kissing people along the way. They were all looking at Juan and wondering who was he and how long would he be with Jon? Jon's reputation for loving and leaving them was notorious. His theme song was really fitting. So most people never even asked the name of the new conquest because the next time they saw Jon, he would be with a new lover or on the prowl for a new triumph. Needless to say, Jon would pass many of his exploits on his way out the door. Some were cordial; others were not. It made no difference to Jon, he was only interested in his own pleasure most of the time. However, for some odd reason things seemed different with Juan; he lived in New York could that be the enticement. Regardless, the real reason was that Jon knew Juan would be soon be gone.

Ignoring malicious comments Jon walked through a contingency of faggots that could make the gayest man want to turn straight. Jon did not like the bottom feeder homosexuals; effeminate, snap queens, drag queens and all the other degenerates of the homosexual community.

Jon loved the homosexual community as a whole, but found it difficult to embrace factions. Being gay did not or will it ever mean wanting to be a woman, dressing like a woman or acting like a woman. Gay meant wanting to love and make love with a person of the same sex. Jon could not fathom anyone wanting to be with any of those dregs.

Past the faggot horde Jon stopped in the middle of the busy street and kissed Juan thankful, that he was not a part of the sissy circle. Holding Juan in the middle of the street a car zoomed pass full of young men.

"Die of AIDS, faggots! Die of AIDS, faggots!" screamed a young man in the passing car.

"Cock Suckers! Butt Fuckers!" yelled another young man from another passing car.

"Come back and say it to my face, fucking assholes!" Jon screamed.

"Jon don't bother. If they weren't afraid of their own sexuality they would not feel the need to yell and scream obscenities," Juan said trying to calm Jon.

"I know, but it just pisses me the fuck off when these bastards yell shit out the windows flying by like maniacs!"

"Don't let that shit get to you. You just have to let it roll off your back and move on. I learned a long time ago not to let stupid shit bother you. It's not worth the effort. Now, come here gimme some tongue."

"I know you're right. Sometimes that crap just push my buttons. I've been working on it, but that shit just pisses me the fuck off! Come here! I thought you asked for something?" Jon said pulling Juan closer to him.

Standing beside Jon's car they kissed. On the ride home Jon passed the sack and matchbook to Juan. He put the white powder in the matchbook corner and under Jon's nose. Sniffing the white powder Jon closed his eyes, momentarily. Opening his eyes, he swerved to miss a car in the other lane.

"Jon! Damn, are you okay to drive? If not I can take the wheel. I don't want to end up dead in Orlando!" Juan screamed.

"Damn!" Jon snapped. "I'm straight. Just sit tight and be cool," Jon said, restrained. Whizzing down Orange Blossom Trail, Juan put the matchbook cover and powder to his nose and took a sniff. They rode down the OBT, music blaring. They passed a police car, Jon looked in the rear view mirror to make sure that the cop didn't turn in pursuit. The police car continued down the trail in the opposite direction. The coke and the alcohol were taking their toll on Jon; he was not as coherent as he usually was after a night of coking and drinking. They made their route to Jon's place. Once inside they did some more coke and had another cocktail before retiring to the bedroom. The night was full of passion. They made love and slept wrapped in each others arms.

Saturday, August 6, 1988

Jon opened his eyes. Juan lay next to him in his bed. Looking around the room for condoms, Jon realized that there were no used ones on the floor or in the wastebasket next to the bed. He looked at Juan, examining his body looking to see if he could detect any signs of HIV/AIDS. There was no way that you can tell by looking if a person has been exposed the HIV virus that causes AIDS. Jon's inspection was in vain. Jon thought that if Juan was HIV positive; he would have told him. He did not seem to be the type of man that would knowingly pass along the virus. Jon remembered that night a while back when he had a one night stand with this guy and the next morning the guy left a note stating welcome to the hell that is AIDS'. Testing and testing and more HIV testing. Negative. Negative and more negative test results. That guy was cool, also. Since there was no definitive HIV/AIDS detection point on the body it was difficult to detect by sight, even by the so called trained professionals.

Jon went to the bathroom. He knew he had to broach the HIV/AIDS subject sometime during the day. Now he had to decide the best approach as not to offend Juan, but he also wanted to bring the matter to the table. AIDS was a menacing topic. Research and more research was needed to find a cure, vaccine or more medicine to eradicate this plague. HIV/AIDS infected thousands of young talented men and women. The disease often sets in before a diagnosis is made.

Crying in the bathroom, Jon sat on the floor trying to make some sense of it all. Why was he so self-destructive? This query plagued Jon, so he did any and everything to escape pondering his life. From all appearances everything seemed good. A good job that paid well, a supportive family and a circle of good friends.

Why did Jon feel so. . . alone and desperate? Maybe that was why his relationships never worked; because he never felt he deserve to be happy with someone. That could have been the real reason for his notorious behavior with lovers. He was looking to his lovers for something that he could not find in himself. When they did not possess it, he discarded them. The only problem was that Jon did not know what he was looking for; so that made the lover's task of being what he needed just that more difficult.

Not having the time for introspection, Jon composed himself. Leaving the bathroom, his personal saga behind, Jon crawled back into bed with Juan. Sensing his return, Juan moved to snuggle up close to Jon. The clock on the dresser displayed ten o 'clock. Much of the morning was gone and Jon wanted to get to the beach. Sleeping cradled in Jon's arm Juan slept like a little kitten nibbling at his mother's nipple. Jon lay there and watch him sleep and thought how great it would be to always have him here just like this morning. Quiet and loving me.

30

"Wake up sleepy head. Wake up baby. We need to get up, if we plan to make it to the beach today. This is your last day in Florida before heading back to the Big Apple. I want to run with you on the sandy shores of sunny Florida. I want you to experience the beach for the first time with me. So when you think of your Florida vacation, and you will, I will be all that you remember. You and me on the sunny shores of Florida," Jon said dancing around the room like a hula dancer.

"You and I on the sunny shores of Florida will not be the way I remember you or my vacation. I will remember a handsome copper tone man with curly short cropped hair and a cheery smile and a big. . . heart. You will be in all of my thoughts until I see you again," Juan said in a groggy thicker Puerto Rican voice.

"Are you game for the beach today? I have a picnic basket, a couple of bottles of wine and some fruit. I know that I got you, but I need something more to nibble."

"Yeah, that sounds like a lot of fun. I don't usually swim, "Jaws" and all, but I will get out there with you. I know that you will protect me from the Mr. Killer Shark. Ain't that right, Jon. You would protect me . . . right?" Juan asked teasing.

"Baby, when it comes to killer sharks, every man for himself and God for us all. Ah, don't worry we'll just give that ole shark a bump and he'll be our friend to the end"

"A bump would really get me up and at 'em!" Juan declared.

"Let's get a shower before we bump."

"Okay." Juan said solemnly.

They took showers and prepared for their day in the sun. Juan and Jon were like school kids on a field trip. Making sure they had all the essential ingredients for a wonderful day they went through the contents of the picnic basket and cooler, twice.

Jon checked to make sure they had enough coke for a day at the beach. To place an order because he knew that the day would consume the powdery substance that remained, Jon called Eric. More coke was needed for Juan's final night in Jon's arms. Jon needed more coke. Eric did not answer. Jon left a message.

On the drive to the beach, Jon and Juan listened to music and talked. Their conversation was about everything, but nothing of substance. Their talk did not give any indication to the inner workings of either man. They arrived at the beach, found a spot put, their blanket and other fun in the sun items down and were off to frolic in the water. They listened to music, drank wine, ate fruit, snorted some cocaine and had a great day at the beach.

Drained from the sun, they walked into Jon's apartment, put everything away and crashed, Juan on the sofa. Jon sat on the floor between the coke table and the sofa. Drifting off to sleep they dreamed of their beautiful day together.

Waking up, Jon looked at the clock that displayed ten o 'clock. Jumping up, he called Eric again. There was no answer. He wondered where Eric was. Pulling out an address book he paged Eric.   In the meantime, he looked through his book to find Monica's number. She had some good blow connections, also. He really didn't like to deal with her, but in a pinch she would have, to.   There was a knock at the door; it was Eric. Going straight to the kitchen, harried Eric made a drink.

"Do you want a cocktail?" Eric asked Jon.

"Yeah, I think I will have a cocktail. Let me wake Juan so we can get ready for tonight," Jon said walking over to Juan.

"Wake up slumber boy. We have company," Jon whispered.

Jon caressed Juan's back and shoulders. He moved gently from Jon's touch. Juan rolled over and opened his eyes narrowly. Looking into his eyes he pulled Jon to him. He leaned over and kissed Juan. He pulled Juan up from the sofa. Juan realized they had a guest. He excused himself to the bedroom.

"What's up, man, you seem a bit wired? Is everything okay?" Jon asked concerned.

"I'm cool. Jus' had a explosion wit my girl and I'm pissed. So I had to squash it. But I got your messages earlier. I ain't have time to come by," Eric said as he calmed from the alcohol.

"Well, me and my boy was at the beach. So we would not have been around this afternoon, anyhow. I'm glad you got the beeps and my bumps," Jon said reaching into his pocket for money.

"Yo, man you a cool fag. I mean gay dude. No disrespect. Jus' habit. We cool."

"Man, why I got be a faggot . . . damn. What's with all that. I am just a Black gay man. 'Aight, no disrespect taken. Cool. Now that we got that out of the way, is shit any good?"

"Should be that same quality as before."

"Well, I'll get the plate and meet you at the table. Hold on, let me get Juan."

Juan met Jon in the hallway. They went to the living room where Eric waited. Putting the plate on the table Jon sat next to Eric on the sofa. Eric gave Jon the triangular bag. He opened the bag to taste its contents. He licked his finger and rubbed his gums. Closing his eyes to feel the surge of coke induced adrenaline rush through his body. Holding his nose he took a deep breath allowing the coke into his head. Juan and Eric waited for Jon's assessment of the powder.

"This some powerful shit!" Jon said.

"Well let's get wit it," Juan said as he reached for the plate.

"I'll cut it and make us some fat lines. Then we can get ready for the club if that is cool with you. Tonight is your last night in Orlando and I want you to have a great time. So, tell me what do you want to do tonight? Besides the blow?" Jon said to Juan.

"Right now just cut it and give a few thick lines and I'll decide what I want the night to hold in store for me," Juan said to Jon.

"Well look like you two got something to do I'll just be like the wind and blow. A corny line, but it's effective," Eric joked.

The threesome laughed at Eric's trite line.

"And on that note I'm outy," Eric said as he headed for the door.

"It was cool to meet you. Hope to see again sometime," Juan said to Eric.

"Yeah, if I'm ever in the Big Apple I'll look you up, and Jon, be cool man. I'll git up wit you later."

"Aight Eric be cool. And man stop that bullshit with your girl, man. You know it ain't right. It just ain't cool. Peace!"

Alone, Jon and Juan sat on the sofa and did a few lines of cocaine. They sat and drank, not speaking for what seemed an eternity. Then came the moment of truth or dare and Jon wanted only the truth. They sat facing each other just looking into the other's eyes.

"I know we've only been together for a few days, but I have grown to really care for you. I wish that we could have more time together. Unfortunately, I'll be on a plane tomorrow bound for New York City. I'm gonna miss you, Jon."

"Yeah, Babe, I wish we had more time, too. Since we don't, let's make the best of it. There is one thing that I think we need to talk about. Remember last night we made love and it was perfect. You are my best lover. You made me feel things I have never felt before. The one thing about last night that harassed me all day is that we didn't use any protection. The last time I was tested, about year ago I was negative, but I have had other nights like last night. No condoms, but great sex. That worries me and that you have not mentioned it, terrifies me. Since you haven't said anything about it that makes my mind wander in all types of directions," Jon expressed genuine care and concern.

"What are you saying? You think I got AIDS? Do you think I would knowingly have unprotected sex if I had AIDS? What kinda person do you think I am?"

"That's just it I don't know what kinda person you are, I don't know you and you don't know me!. I would hope that you wouldn't have sex with me knowing that you have AIDS and not say anything. Last night we did, without discussion about status. I'm just as guilty. I never asked and you didn't say anything. We just . . . did it."

"I'm sorry, you're right you don't know me and I don't know you. We should have talked about something before I gave myself to you. I just thought that if there was something you needed to tell me that you would. Because that is how I am. No, I don't have AIDS and I'm not HIV positive."

"Neither am I," Jon said reassuringly .

Reaching out to Juan he pulled him close. Holding Juan and gently caressing his face and kissed him. Their lips met and tenderly touched again and again. They made love,raw, without protection. More coke. More sex. More alcohol. More coke. More sex. More alcohol.

The rain began to sprinkle on the street. Jon and his buddies ran to avoid the rain. Everybody ran home except Jon and Cecil. They ran to the utility shed in Jon's backyard. They were there just shooting the shit. They talked about school, the football team, the band and other topics of interest to high school kids. In the shed Jon acknowledged something about himself; he liked to spend time with guys. He wanted to feel touch Cecil's body. He didn't exactly know what was happening, but he knew that this was not right.

Jon continued talking with Cecil in the shed and turned to conversation to sex; sexual positions and masturbation. Then the unexpected happened Cecil asked to see Jon's member to compare size. His mind racing, not knowing what was going to transpire, Jon unzipped his pants, as did Cecil. They stood there with their members exposed. Each touched and explored the other's member with innocence and curiosity.

Jon and Cecil departed after the exploration. Inside Jon pondered his activities. Jon knew that there was something different about him, but he didn't know what. He liked girls and had girlfriends, but he always had this attraction to guys. This was his first male sexual encounter, but it definitely would not be his last.

Since there were no gay men in town that Jon could talk to about his experience, he just kept it to himself. He found himself looking for ways to be around Cecil more and more. He enjoyed the naive sexual interlude and did it again on other occasions, then things changed.

To Jon's chagrin Cecil told some neighborhood boys about their sexual interlude and did not want to spend time with Jon anymore. Of course, Cecil's story was different from the truth. No matter. Jon continued to play basketball, football and other activities with neighborhood guys. The relationship with Cecil was severed forever. The neighborhood boys didn't react any differently to Jon than before, so life went on as it had in Jon's small home town. Unbeknownst to Jon there was a difference from the neighborhood boys, but they never showed him their ugly side. Behind Jon's back the boys called him faggot, sissy, punk and any other derogatory homosexual reference imaginable.

One hot afternoon, Jon was invited to Matt's house to look at some Playboy magazines. When he arrived Matt told him to come into his bedroom to make sure no one saw them with his father's magazines. They looked at a few and Jon was getting excited, but he concealed his excitement with the magazine. Matt sensed they both were getting turned on.

"If you show me your thang I'll show you mine," Matt said.

"Why? I don' wanna to see your dick," Jon said.

"Why you wanna act like that wit me. Cecil told us that you like to suck dick and mine is bigger than his. So here suck it," Matt said pushing himself toward Jon face.

"What the hell. Git your funky ass dick outta my face. What is your problem?" Jon said pushing Matt away from him.

"I don't know what Cecil told you and I really don't give a damn, but let me git out your damn house before I have to kick off in your ass?" Jon yelled as he headed for the door.

"What kinda fag is you, don't wanna suck a brothas' dick?"

"The kind that don't wanna have nothing to do wit you, fucker," Jon said as he slammed the front door of Matt's house.

Walking home Jon realized that his life was not going to be the same. Now when ever someone wanted to hang out, why did they really want to hang out? Jon was upset that Cecil's story had now made him the target for the neighborhood young men's sexual cravings. He did not know that they would be as bold, as Matt, to ask him to service their penis. Life in his small town had changed and not for the better. Cecil had made his life difficult.

That was the first time that Jon's emotions were crushed by another man. Jon vowed that he would never put his emotions in the hands of another man, ever. Cecil and Jon did not have a relationship, but that was the catalyst for Jon developing a hardcore fuck'em and leave'em attitude. His notorious reputation was built from the rubble of his shattered emotions, when he was betrayed by Cecil, at fourteen. Jon never thought much about Cecil or his shattered heart. He just remained true to his vow never to put his emotions in the hand of a man, ever.

Anita Baker's voice filled the room with her sweet essence. They lay there on sweat drenched sheets holding each other passionately. Their nakedness gleamed with sensuality in the shadows of candle light. Around midnight, they were startled by pounding at the door. Jumping out of bed grabbing his bath robe, Jon went to the door to see who was there. It was Eric. Standing there with a menacing look on his face. Jon opened the door to let Eric enter.

"Jon, man I'm tired of that bitch. She was on me again and I just had to leave. Sorry that I came busting up your action. I just needed to get away from her for a few. Do you mind if I make myself a drink?" Eric asked exhausted.

"Have I ever stopped you before. Women ain't nothing but trouble. I don't know what ya'll arguing about and I don't want to know. Kelli seems like a nice young woman. Hard working and wants something out of life. I know that she does not approve of your occupation. Don't run that line a brotha gotta get paid. I get paid. My job doesn't require me out all time of night with all sorts of people. If you care about that girl at all stop whatcha doin' and get a job. You are a smart young man and you have a great deal of potential. I'm sure if you wanted to turn your life around, Kelly would be there for you. You gotta do what you gotta do."

"Damn, man why you got to be all on that tip, with Kelly. I know deep down she is right. If I want something out of life I know I got to get off the streets and into a profession. I know I can't do it by myself. However, I'm gonna have to cut her loose. 'Cause I'm gon' be in the game for a few more years stashing my flow. If she don't want to take the ride I can't force her, but I gotta do it for a few more years and I'm outy. If she don't want to deal wit she can step."

"Do you love her Eric? If you do try to see things from her point of view."

"Love, like Tina Turner say, What's love got to with it. Yeah, I do care 'bout her but I need the flow to treat her right. Without the flow what I got to give her. Nothing but a hard life."

"Have you ever thought that she loves you and not the money you give her. Kelli wants to be with you, the man, not for who you are, but for who you can become. She sees that you are a good man and they are hard to come by I know. Kelly don't want to throw it away on account of money. Take your time and think it through entirely. Do not make a mistake that you will regret."

"Thanks man, I know I'm all up in your business, but thanks for the talk. I really 'preciate it." Eric said genuinely.

"I'm all right my brotha, stay strong, be cool. Peace."

Eric left without ever making his drink leaving Jon to ponder his own situation. Feeling like a hypocrite, giving advice to someone about getting their life together. He sat on the sofa and thought about where his life was and where he wanted it to go. Trying to keep everything in perspective he began to take stock of his life.

Jon looked at his failed personal relationships and strained family ties. This is not the way he envisioned his life at twenty-seven. By now he should have accomplished more with his life. He is educated, has a decent work ethic and enjoys life. Why were the things that would make his life complete just out of touch of his out stretched hand?

Introspection is a good thing. Looking inward to find his answers, Jon tried to construct his life from the beginning. Where did it all begin? How had his life gotten so out of control? Jon didn't know the answers to his questions and a part of him didn't want to find any resolution. There was the part of him that needed to know the reason for all the sex, drugs and alcohol. What made him want to self-destruct? Was it the fact that he never had the relationship with his father that he wanted as a child? Maybe it the way he was potty trained? Jon did not know.

He sat there for over an hour just thinking about some of the things he'd encountered in his life. The times he would never forget and those that he wished he could forget. He had a good life on the surface, but beneath all the fun lies the truth. He just wanted to be loved. Not the love of a mother or father but that of a lover.

The love of a lover was always at Jon's fingertips. He traipsed to the bedroom and Juan folded into his arms. He was a perfect fit. This was what Jon wanted; all was good with the world. The reality was that this was what Jon wanted ... someone who didn't live in his city so he could continue being notorious in the game of amour.

Tonight was Juan's last night in Orlando before heading back to New York. Sitting in bed they talked. This was the first time that they really just sat and talked about life, their ambitions, desires and goals. Neither felt inhibited or afraid to share his innermost thoughts and feelings about the future or their fears. Jon shared his story about how Cecil betrayed him and about life in a small town. Juan shared the story about his first lover that was killed in a drug bust.

The night moved slowly as they shared more stories about life and love in the past and looked to the future. That maybe there was a chance for the two of them to forge a relationship. They both thought about a relationship for about a minute and decided that the distance if nothing else would kill the relationship. Jon and Juan both admitted that they had shared more with each other that night than they ever shared with any other person they were involved with. Being with each other talking made both of them feel a special bond. Secrets that were shared would only strengthen their friendship and, if by some twist of fate one day, a relationship. A real relationship built on trust and mutual respect. Their conversation lasted for three hours when they realized that there was only about two hours before Juan needed to be at the hotel with his family. Juan really enjoyed spending his last night in Orlando with Jon. Jon felt the same.

They made love for the final time before Juan's departure from Orlando. Love making for them was an art form. Their bodies moved in unison. For them, making love was like ballet, poised and exquisite. Tonight, making love was serene. No coke. No alcohol. Making love was pure. They lay in bed damp from genuine passion, not wet from lust. The room smelled of male love; the aroma penetrated their nostrils and made them smile. Jon held Juan so close he felt his heartbeat. Jon knew this was the last time he would make love with Juan and he did not want the night to end.

Sunday, August 7, 1988

Juan and Jon kissed their last goodbye. They made their way to the door of Jon's apartment. Stopping at the door, Jon held Juan one more time. This was it. Jon opened the door for Juan and they left for the hotel. On the drive they both talked about the next time they would be together. Jon had already planned a New York trip to spend time with Juan. Arriving at the hotel they embraced. Jon made an impression on the family; they liked him immediately. The kids asked him all sorts of questions about living in Florida, everything from did he wrestle alligators to did he really like orange juice.

"Do you go to the beach all year round?" asked Juan's niece.

"How do you know my Uncle Juan? Are you from the Brooklyn?" questioned Juan's nephew.

"I'm sorry, they are just so curious about everything.

41

Questions all day and night. They never stop asking questions. Enough asking questions! Leave him alone," Lysette yelled at the kids.

"Not a problem. I love kids and they generally like me. I'm fine," Jon said honestly.

"Juan, a one that likes kids. That's a good sign. Now if we can only get him to Brooklyn," Lysette teased Juan.

All the adults laughed. They kids were now tuned into a cartoon on television. Jon said his goodbyes to the family and went to the door. Juan followed and walked with him to his car. They stood there and just looked at each other until Jon had to leave. Because if he didn't leave at that very moment he wouldn't have left.

Jon was meeting friends for brunch after early morning service. Church was church, nothing extraordinary, nothing major. Just another Sunday morning and the Reverend making points about how to live a righteous life. The Reverend tried to help his congregation avoid the pits of hell, the fiery furnace. He preached from Matthew, Mark, Luke or some other Bible book boy. The sermon topic was *Recognize the Wolf in Sheep's Clothing*. Jon really didn't get too much from the sermon. He had a problem with organized religion, but he went in hope that one Sunday the preacher would recognize spirituality and a personal relationship with the Higher Power. Besides, many Black ministers preached that all homosexuals were going to hell, anyway. Jon rallied in his personal relationship with the Higher Power and could care less about anyone's opinion of him or his sexuality.

Still pondering the righteousness of it all Jon arrived at "the cafe". He looked around the cafe to find his brunch companions. As Jon approached the table he realize that Ernest was with Cyril and Bruce and thought this should be quite interesting.

"Have you guys been waiting long? Church ran a little longer than usual. Sorry," Jon said apologetically.

"Yeah, yeah I'm sure that it was the long service that held you up. When was that boy leaving? I'm sure he didn't have anything to do with you being late for brunch, now did he?" Cyril questioned in ethnic vernacular.

"You are so wrong. Juan's plane left hours ago. Thank you very much. I took him back to the Peabody where his sister stayed for the week. Otherwise, he would be right here with me, now!" Jon boasted.

"Oh really now, would he be right here wit'cha, now?" Ernest asked solemnly.

"Well, yeah I would have brought him with me. We've done everything together since we met Thursday. Sorry, but he would have been here," Jon stated frankly.

"So it's like that, huh. Fuck me, don't call me or nothing. Damn! Now I know why they call you the Notorious Knight. I knew I should have never took you home with me," Ernest stated candidly.

"You're right, because if you thought it was more than just what it was, then you made a mistake. Besides, you could have called me, you had the number. So don't play the martyr role with me. It's not cute on you. With that out of the way, let's eat, I's ravenous," Jon stated without blinking an eye.

"You are cut–throat and ruthless," Cyril said honestly.

"If you can't run with the big dogs . . . you need to stay your ass on the porch and let us run. Now, are we done with this, because if we are not I might need to find somewhere else to eat. The subject is tired and ovah," Jon said directly.

"Well, you are right, I could have called and I didn't. So, you are right, I got exactly what I deserved. Thank you, Jon, you have taught me a valuable lesson. Thanks, I really mean it. Let's eat, I's ravenous, too," Ernest stated sardonically.

"You kids are too much for me," Cyril teased.

"Damn! Jon you are cold-blooded. But, you all right wit me," Bruce said.

"Cool man, but I'm just straight up. I don't play no games.

We can do what we do and move on. If we want to hit again and we both with it, we can do that, too," Jon said nonchalantly.

"What do you mean he's all right with you?" Cyril asked.

"You know that he is straight up and not about bullshit! You know what I mean, Cyril!" Bruce said sternly.

"I'm just checking, but I know he's not about what you want. I thought you knew," sassed Cyril.

"Now, how you know what I'm about? Do you know?" Jon question.

"Oh, believe me I know. Do you forget who you talking to? Now don't have me bring it all back to your memory," Cyril joked.

"I don't have the foggiest idea what you are talking about?" Jon said.

"Now, I know it's been a whole lotta boys, but remember that one night you and Marvin when we were in Miami for the weekend," Cyril paused.

"Say no more. Okay. You know enough," Jon laughed.

"Who's Marvin?" Bruce asked.

"No one of importance. Just someone that we don't talk about. Right Cyril," Jon said candidly.

"Yeah, we don't talk about Marvin," Cyril said laughing.

"Come on who is Marvin? You have got to tell us something," Ernest asked.

"There's nothing to tell. Waiter. Thanks, I'll have the cheesy omelette with extra mushrooms," Jon ordered.

In Jon's usual style he moved the conversation away from the topic and moved on to other interesting morsels. Bruce became the topic of conversation.

"So, what is your deal, Bruce? Don't play that game with me that you don't know what I'm talking about, either." Jon said.

"Look Jon, I don't care who you do. So don't care who I do," Bruce said frankly.

"Don't go there, Jon. This is not the time or place. It really isn't any of your business.I know that were are close friends, but don't go there," Cyril said through clenched teeth.

"I just always wanted to know why gay men got married and continued the gay lifestyle. It has just always amazed me. One, because if you are gay, leave women alone. Don't pull women into your fucked up drama. Two, Poor gay boys allow themselves to get sucked into your twisted way of life. I just never understand any of it. I never did," Jon frankly stated.

"Look man, like I said before. Do what you do and don't worry about me, cool," Bruce told Jon.

"I just wanted a little clarification, but if I can't get it at this table, no problem," Jon blankly stated, as he waved his hands in mock surrender.

Brunch was going great. Jon had managed to irritate everyone at the table and he'd only been there for ten minutes. Ernest and Bruce excused themselves to have a smoke. Cyril and Jon were left at the table. The waiter brought over a tray with two mimosas for Cyril and Jon. They sat and drank in silence.

Cyril just could not believe Jon would bring up the subject of gay married men, knowing that Bruce was married. Cyril thought of all the time and energy that he'd invested in his relationship with Bruce. He knew that the relationship could go no further than where it was. The more Cyril thought about his situation, the more annoyed he became. He began to look at his relationship, if you could call it that. The more he thought, the more the truth came flooding to the forefront. Cyril realized that he did not have a relationship and he was cheating with someone's husband and father. Nevertheless, Cyril did not stop dating Bruce at brunch that warm Sunday morning. Bruce and Ernest returned from their smoke just as the omelettes were being served. The brunch companions bowed their heads for the blessing. The food was exceptional. The chef had really outdone himself today with the cheesy omelette special.

The quartet ate in silence. Music from a local radio station washed over the cafe in waves. The only other sound was from forks and knives against china and the rustle of linen. Bruce sat and looked at Cyril for a sign. Jon needed no sign. Ernest ate, clueless to the interaction at the table. Brunch was over and the quartet disbanded. The single gay man Cyril and the married gay man Bruce left together. Single searching for love Ernest left alone, too. Jon went to the bar for another mimosa.

Sitting at the bar Jon began to talk with the bartender, an attractive Black man with braided jet black hair and two silver hoop earrings. Jon did not know where this would lead. He didn't even know if the man was gay, not that it mattered. Jon continued with innuendo and blatant flirtation. They talked for the rest of afternoon. Ian's shift ended.

"So, what's up? What's on your agenda for the rest of today?" Jon asked Ian.

"Laundry and I need to run errands. After that I'm open," Ian said.

"You want to get together later after you've finished?"

"That could be fun. Let's say I give you a ring when I'm finished and you can give me directions to your flat. How does that sound?"

"Sounds great. Here's my card. I look forward to hearing from you tonight."

"I'll see you soon."

"I'll wait to hear from you before I do anything. I hope that you will give me a ring tonight."

"Until tonight," Ian said as he left "the cafe". The phone rang at Jon's apartment; he decided to let the answering machine pick up instead of taking the call. Juan left a message.

"Just called to let you know that we got home safe and everything. I know that it has only been a day, but I miss you. I don't know if I can sleep without being in your arms. I can't wait until you come up here. You have been on my mind all day. I just can't stop thinking about you. Hope that we can maintain our friendship and . . . you know. Well, call me when you get the message. I can't wait to hear from you. I'll be talking to you. Bye. I'll talk at you, soon. This is so lame I need to just hang up the phone, but I'm hoping that you will come in while I'm talking to your machine. Then you could pick up and I could hear your voice . . . Okay, I see you're not home. Call me, goodbye," Juan left his message.

Jon sat in the living room contemplating his own troubles. He was at a crossroads with his life. He didn't know why his life was so messed up or what he needed to do to make it all better. Everything seemed to be getting out of control and he needed the control back. How could he gain control over his unyielding decadent craving.

"I want some candy! I want some candy!" Jon screamed.

Jon never learned self-control. He remembered how when he was little, he always got what he wanted, when he wanted it. He never did without. His parents did everything in their power to make sure that he longed for nothing. Jon was a spoiled brat and he knew it.

That was the catalyst for his insatiable yearning for what he desired. Relationships were a lark, because he never could find anyone to live up to his perfect standards for a lover. He wanted his lover to worship the ground he walked upon and if he said the sky was purple, they believed him without question.

The only problem with Jon's perfect lover syndrome was when someone acquiesced, he thought they were weak and unworthy of his attention. They would never feel his love. Jon's ideal lover would challenge him on every turn and not just accept what he said as gospel. He had not run into that type often. On occasion when he did, they never lived where he lived and he didn't do long distance relationships well.

There was a knock at the door. Jon recoiled himself from his thoughts to see who interrupted his introspection. To his surprise, it was Ian. Jon was perplexed. He had not given Ian directions to his apartment complex. Jon invited Ian to have a seat.

"I'm sorry that I arrived this way, without warning. I know I was supposed to give you a ring, but I just decided to come on over. You did say that you would do nothing until you heard from me?"

"I did. I thought I would give you directions. I would receive a ring. I'm not accustomed to people just dropping over, without calling first. How did you get here?" Jon asked bewildered.

"I'm sorry. A friend works for a delivery service. There is one directory that lists everybody in Orlando, by name, address and/or phone number. Your full name was on the card. If I've interrupted something I can always call and come by later?" Ian said rakishly.

"Oh, that wouldn't make any sense. Stay you're here already. Can I make you a drink? I'm having Tanqueray on the rocks with lime. What would you like? This feels weird making a cocktail for a mixologist," Jon said not as perplexed.

"I sensed that you are a little put off by my forward demeanor. I do apologize for not ringing you as we planned. That mistake will not happen, again. I'm not really a bartender. Friends, own the cafe and their bartender called in sick and Geoffrey was away on holiday. Geoffrey is one of the owners. So Ethan called me in a panic. I told that I would assist for the brunch shift. I really am a systems analyst for IBM. I will have the same, if you don't have Beefeater's?"

"Tanqueray, it is then."

"I just love your paintings. Are they originals? I don't recognize the artist."

"Yes, they are. The artist is a frat brother. I always encouraged him to pursue his art and he gave me some of his work for encouraging him."

"I like the dark brooding colors in these one. I like anything that represents the dark, moody side of people. What is the title?"

"He calls it Noir. He titled it Noir to declare his passion for film noir of the 30's and 40's.

He thinks himself a film buff," Jon joked.

"I'm really impressed with his work. Has he had a showing?"

"Yeah, a few here and there. Some of his stuff is on display at the Orlando Museum of Art in their emerging artist series. He also has some paintings at the African-American Gallery of Art here in Orlando."

"I didn't even know there was an African-American Gallery of Art in Orlando? Where is it located? "

"I'm not sure about the address, but it right across the street from the community center downtown, not the one at the O-rena. I can't remember, but an artist named Everett Spruill is the owner."

"I'd really like to pop over to see what type of art work he has. What are his hours?"

"I'm not really sure but I think he's open in the evenings until about 8:30 or 9:00. But, I could be mistaken. Well . . .the last time I was at his gallery he told me he was considering an offer to become the curator of a museum in Georgia, I think. He's probably still here, though,"

"I hope he is still here. I dabbled in art when I was tot growing up in Antigua, finger painting."

"I was never artistically inclined but I did play an instrument in the high school band."

"Really, what instrument?"

"I played trumpet. And when I played at my high school graduation that was the last time I blew an instrument. Being in the band was a lotta fun," Jon reminisced.

"You really enjoyed the high school band?"

"I did."

"So, what type of music do you have here?"

"I have an eclectic music library. Take a peek and find something you like and put it on. I need to go the bathroom."

"I'll just do that."

Ian turned out to be a Nona Hendrix fan. Jon had taped a couple of her albums. Ian put the tape in and turned up the volume. He began to rock out to *Transformation*. He danced around the living room examining everything. He was impressed with the artwork and furnishings in Jon's apartment. Jon returned from the bathroom and stood in the kitchen watching Ian dance before he joined in on the fun. They danced for the remainder of the tape.

"Whew, I'm a little winded. What other type of music do you get into? I have a pretty good selection. I'll make us some more drinks."

"Well, I did see another lady I really get into, how about some Janis Ian."

"I just love her *At Seventeen*. I really could relate to it when I was a teenager."

"I really started to listen to because of her last name. Then I listened to her prolific lyrics and I was captivated. Her storytelling is impeccable. I just adore *In Winter*. You can feel the desperation of the lady in the song. How her life is so desolate and her former lover's blissful. That song always make me feel melancholy," Ian whispered.

"I know, her lyrics are so seriously devoid of hope. Her life outlook is despair and loneliness. Like I said before, I can relate. Before I would sink into depression, I'd usually put on some dance music to lift my spirits. Her lyrics are moving and powerful, but they can be a downer."

"Janis Ian it is and then a some Tina Turner to add a little spice to things."

"I can think of other ways to spice things up."

"What do you mean?"

"Come on over here and find out."

"Um, I have a lover and I don't think he would like that too much."

"You have a lover. And. What does that mean?"

"It means that I am faithful to my relationship and I don't fuck around."

"Then what have we been doing all evening?"

"Well I been having a wonderful time hanging out with a new friend. I thought that was what you were doing also?"

"Yeah, right. Hanging out. . .with a new friend."

"Come here and give us a big hug. Jon, you are my new friend and I don't want anything to jeopardize my friendship or my relationship. You do understand, don't you?"

Jon went across the room to give Ian a big hug. He was not too pleased with the direction the evening had taken. Walking across the room, Jon's mind was flooded with questions. How did he read Ian so wrong? How could he get Ian out, so he can hit the club to find a conquest? He needed another cocktail and some coke because this was turning into a long, drawn-out evening and it was only 9:00 p.m. He reached Ian standing with out-stretched arms. They embraced. There was an undeniable intense spark of excitement between the two of them. Both of them felt the overwhelming passion when their bodies connected. Jon stepped away from Ian. Jon stood there astonished. Ian walked to the kitchen and made more drinks. He walked out of the kitchen leaving the drinks on the counter.

"I'm sorry, Jon, I forgot the drinks in the kitchen," Ian said worriedly rubbing his temples.

"I'll get them. Don't worry about it."

"I just completely forgot why I was in the kitchen, so I came back to the living room. Of course, then I remembered."

"Here's your drink."

"Thank you."

"Not a problem. Now, I can't let it just go like that. Did you feel something when we hugged? I felt this surge of adrenaline and I mean, I'm reeling from just your touch. I know that you felt something. Didn't you?"

"I didn't feel a thing. Sorry Jon, but I think I need to be going now!"

"I know you need to get home so I will talk with you later."

Ian finished his drink and headed for the door. Jon followed him. They glanced at each other, both afraid to look the other in the eye, afraid of what they would see. He reached to give Ian a hug before they departed. When their bodies touched, the passion overcame them and they kissed.

"What am I doing? Enrique would not understand. Hell, I don't understand. Jon, what have you done to me?"

"What have I done to you? Nothing. What have you done to me? I have this uncontrollable desire to kiss your mouth and devour your body, but I know that you have another. This does not happen to me. This is just an infatuation. I know that it can't go any further. You know it can't go any further. I have to admit I've never felt this intense about anyone in my entire life. Okay, it was the drinks, our talk about art, music and the dancing. We just got caught up in the moment. This will pass. You need to leave now. Otherwise, I will not be responsible for my actions. I want so badly for you. I want to hold you and kiss you and have you close to me."

"Jon, I can't leave. I have to stay. I need to stay. I'll take my chances with you. I have this mischievous urge to kiss you, hold you and feel your body pressed against mine."

"I need another drink. Would you like one?"

"No, right now all I need is to be with you!"

"Okay, the drink can wait. Come here."

"I'll meet you midway. I can hardly wait."

They met in the middle of the living room. Jon pulled Ian to him. He kissed him and Ian kissed him back. Ian caressed Jon's shoulders as they kissed. Jon held Ian so close. Moving slowly to the floor, Jon and Ian knelt facing each other. Jon's eyes pierced Ian to his very soul. Ian captured the true essence of passion when he looked into Jon's eyes. The desire between Ian and Jon was brilliant. They consumed each other.

Jon thought that he and Juan had made love like no others made love before. He was wrong. He and Ian made love that was pristine, impeccable and tremendous. He had just made love with another man's lover. This was nothing new for Jon, but for the first time in a long time, he felt. For so many years

DETACHED

Jon hid his emotions so deep inside that nothing and no one could penetrated to those depths. Ian had not penetrated that deeply, but there was an opening, a sliver.

Around midnight, Ian looked at the clock. He should have been home hours ago. Ian had to go home. He moved to get out of bed; Jon pulled him back. They embraced and kissed. Ian removed himself from the bed. Watching Ian prepare to leave broke Jon's spirit. He didn't know what to say or do. His mind raced a thousand miles a minute, never leaving the bedroom. He wondered what would happen next. Would he ever experience the love he shared with Ian again? The question plagued him. That would be the only time Jon and Ian made love.

Jon sat in bed looking like a little boy whose best friend moved away, sad. Ian dressed and was ready to leave. They didn't know what course their intimate liaison would take. Neither wanted the night to end. Ian left.

Jon knew that he would never have Ian in his life so he just put him and their passion out of his mind. He was good at not dealing with the real. That is how he could have so many conquests and never feel anything. Jon turned and twisted in his sleep. He grieved for the love of Ian. He felt bereft. A quiet, gentle slumber would not come tonight for Jon.

Monday, August 8, 1988

Monday morning. The bright sunlight crashed through the blinds like a bull charging a matador. The beams of light stung Jon's eyes as he struggled to wake up. Today was the first day of the rest of his life having experienced pure love. Jon sat in the bed and held Ian's pillow, embracing his essence.

Jon made his way to the kitchen to make coffee. He took the small plate from the cupboard and sniffed cocaine. The smell of fresh brewed coffee filled the air. Eggs, bacon and toast were on Jon's plate for breakfast. He finished breakfast, showered and was off to the office.

Claire was at her desk when Jon arrived at the office. She pulled files for the week. Jon's first client was Mr. Johnson. In the beginning, he was always in a bad mood. He did not feel a need for therapy, but, his wife insisted he get help or she would leave him. Mr. Johnson was from a generation when you did not talk about your feelings, emotions or personal problems publicly. Don't air your dirty laundry in public.

Mr. Johnson would come in once a week to talk. He was at a point in therapy that he could cut back to once a month, but he opted not, to. Jon had spoken with Mrs. Johnson and she was pleased with his progress. Jon and Mr. Johnson talked about sports, movies, politics and other current events. That was Mr. Johnson's therapy. He developed a friendship with Jon and didn't want that to change.

Jon made notations in Mr. Johnson's case file and replaced it in the confidential file cabinet. He sat and read over case notes from his last session with Mr. Adams. Jon's mind began to wander about the events of last night with Ian. He wanted to speak with him, but he did not have a phone number or even his last name. So, Jon called *the cafe*.

"The cafe, this is Geoffrey, how may I assist you?"

"Hello, my name is Jon, I was at *the cafe* yesterday and I met your bartender, Ian. Is he there by chance?"

"Sorry, this is no one working here by that name."

"No, I'm wrong, he doesn't work there, he was helping Ethan yesterday, because the other owner was on holiday and the bartender called in sick. He is a friend of the owners."

"I'm sorry, sir. He's not here. Is there anything else I can do for you? Do you need a reservation?"

"No, I really need to speak with Ian."

"I'm sorry he's not here, sir, but I will let him know that you called. How's that?"

"I guess that will have to do," Jon declared.

"Thank you for calling have a nice day," Geoffrey replied and hung up the phone.

Jon grabbed the telephone directory and frantically looked for an IBM telephone number. He contacted IBM's customer service department, but without a last name he could not be connected with Ian. Jon could not stop thinking about Ian. He had no way of contacting him, so he decided to wait until Ian contacted him. It was not easy for Jon to get Ian out his mind.

The morning passed by at a snail's pace. Jon took a long lunch; after his first afternoon appointment canceled. He went to 4th Fighter for lunch. He ate alone. Ian was still on his mind; he needed a diversion. In the rest room he sniffed a little coke. Sitting looking over the air strip, he drank another glass of zinfandel. Jon decided he needed to put an end to this Ian situation once and for all. He still needed a diversion. The waitress came back to his table to make sure everything was to his satisfaction.

"How is everything, sir?" asked the perky blonde waitress.

"Everything is just fine."

"Sir, are you sure? You look a little. . .; I don't know, I can't put my finger on it. Are you sure everything is all right?"

"Yes Ms., everything is fine."

"Would care for another glass of wine?"

"Yes, I think I will have one more before heading back to the office."

"Can I take these out of your way, sir?" she asked as she reached for the plates.

"Please," he stated. Jon finished his wine, paid his check and was off to the office. On the way to the office he gargled and popped some mints in his mouth. He had a very satisfying lunch. The office was busier that normal for a Monday. He went to his office and briefed himself for his next appointment. Ms. Jones' file was open but Jon's mind wandered. He could not keep Ian out of his thoughts. Ian's presence had become a problem. He only had a few minutes before Ms. Jones' arrival. He said a quick prayer asking the Higher Power to remove this man from his memory so he could function without thoughts of Ian.

Claire buzzed Jon to tell him Ms. Jones had arrived for her appointment. She came into the office and took a seat across from Jon. They exchanged pleasantries. He suggested they move to the other office chairs, they were more comfortable. She followed. Jon began his routine asking her questions about her week. She responded that her week was fine. She had dinner with her sister, they had talked. She had finally been able to meet with her sister to confront her about childhood issues. Ms. Jones' therapy was for classic sibling rivalry, out of control. Talking with her sister was a tremendous step in the right direction for Ms. Jones. Near the end of her session Ms. Jones mentioned not being ready for a relationship. Jon told her they would begin at that point, about not being ready for a relationship, next time. She agreed and left his office.

At his desk, Jon was not thinking about Ian; he reviewed a case file for his next appointment. Isabella Toussaint, Mrs. Bruce Toussaint was his next client she was referred by a colleague. Jon got a fresh legal pad from his supply drawer and readied himself for his appointment. As he read more information from her file he realized who she was. Immediately Jon thought he should exchange the file with another colleague. There was not enough time to make the exchange so he was caught in a precarious situation.

Mrs. Toussaint was Bruce's wife. One of his best friend's boyfriend's wife was about to come into his office for a session. He was a little nervous at first, but then he thought she was there for a session and she was oblivious to the whole Bruce and Cyril situation. The preliminary file notes were from her in-take forms were incomplete. There was no background information to determine why she needed a session. Jon sat and waited for her arrival.

"Mrs. Toussaint is here. Should I send her in?" Claire asked over intercom.

"Please do, thank you, Claire." Jon said into the intercom.

Jon prepared for the door to open to finally see her, Bruce's Missus. He did not know what to expect. The door opened and a 5' 8" beauty stood in his doorway. She was shapely with all the curves in the right places. Her auburn hair gently framed her oval face and her chestnut eyes sparkled. She epitomized beauty.

"Mrs. Toussaint, I'm Jon, I'll be working with you today. I am sorry for the mix-up, but we are together at last."

"Very pleased to meet you Jon and by all means call me Bella. All my friends do and I hope that we can be friends, also."

"Very well, Bella it is. I'm sorry for the mix-up. It has been a madhouse around here lately. We had our quarterly reports were due Friday and a few therapists are still preparing case analysis reports. Why don't we take a seat and get started," Jon apologized sincerely. "We've already established you prefer to be called Bella. Okay, Bella what made you decide to come to therapy today?"

"Well, my husband keeps accusing me of being paranoid."

"Are you paranoid, Bella?"

"I don't think I'm paranoid, just suspicious."

"Suspicious of what exactly?"

"I think my husband is having an affair."

"An affair, what would make you think that?"

Jon's mind whirled. He sat in his office with his best friend's boyfriend's wife. She wondered if her husband was having an affair. Jon knew the answer. He hoped his demeanor would not betray him.

"There is nothing concrete that I can put a finger on, but he just acts strangely, after he's been out with the boys," she confided.

"Strangely? What does he do?"

"Well, he never wants to be with me. He comes in and goes straight to the shower. Then he goes directly to bed. Every now and then we might . . . be intimate, but not usually. When I ask him about his night, he is always vague and never gives me a straight answer."

"What does your husband do out with the boys? Does he go bowling, play darts or shoot pool? Maybe he is tired from his night out with the boys. What night of the week does he usually go out? Maybe that will shed some light on the situation," Jon questioned. "I don't know what he does. But I know alcohol is involved. He doesn't go out on the same night always. One week it is Wednesday, another week its Thursday and some weeks its Wednesday and Friday," she declared.

"Aside from him going out with the boys, what makes you suspect he is having an affair?"

Jon thought besides the fact that he either came home smelling like male sex or Irish Spring fresh.

"Well . . . nothing else really."

"Is there anything else that he does that would make you think that he is being unfaithful?"

"No," she said softly.

"So, because he goes out and wants to go to bed after being out you have concluded that your husband is having an affair?"

"He comes home in such a joyful mood. He's humming and singing and he's never like that with me. So, I have to think there's another woman making him happy. I'm sure as hell not."

"Bella, how long have you been married?"

"We've been married for six years and together for eight."

"During your six years of marriage, to your knowledge, has he ever been unfaithful?"

She shook her head no in response to his question.

"During your time together has he ever done anything that would lead you to believe that he could be unfaithful?"

"No, I don't know what I'm doing here. I have a good husband and two beautiful children. I have the life that most women would kill for. But, my female intuition tells me that he is doing something. I'm crazy I guess."

"No if you are feeling this detachment from your husband you need to discuss the situation with him. Maybe he should not go out as much if it causes you such distress. Do you and your husband spend any time together alone?"

"Not really. We don't have any family here and with all the stories about babysitters, strangers to us, abusing children, we are just leery about leaving our kids with a stranger."

"Maybe you can make a lunch date to talk?" he advised.

"That sounds like a good idea."

"Mrs. Toussaint, why did you really come to my office. You seem to be an intelligent woman and your demeanor indicates that you are here for reasons other that to discuss your alleged paranoia. Especially since you don't exhibit any characteristics of paranoia. Mrs. Toussaint, why are you really here?" Jon asked sternly.

"Like I told you before my husband thinks I'm paranoid." she said sensing Jon's irritation.

"Okay, that is your husband thinking you're paranoid, why are you here instead of your husband?"

"Look I'll bottom line it for you. I was going through my husband's pockets before sending his clothes to the laundry and I found your card!" she said with inexplicable defiance.

"So by finding my card in your husband's pocket, you deduced that he was having an affair? Now how do I figure into the equation?"

Bella stated candidly, "Jon, I know that you're gay."

"And . . . ,"

"You fags are always trying to get a real man! Ya'll will try to steal a woman's husband, a child's father! And you don't care who you hurt in the process. You people will do anything to be with a real man! But, you will never get him! He is mine and he is not, I repeat not going anywhere!" she exclaimed.

"Now we're getting somewhere. So, you think that I am involved with your husband because you found my card in his pocket?" he paused. She gave no response.

"Mrs. Toussaint you are very much mistaken and I am not or have I ever been involved with your husband. You can believe me or not, it doesn't matter. But I do see that you have some real issues with your husband's sexuality. I'm not the right therapist for you. I will make a referral for you and your husband with one of our marriage counselors. If that is what you want? Your marriage appears to be in deep trouble. Now, is your husband bisexual?"

"No, my husband is not bisexual and I don't need an appointment with a marriage counselor. I don't know what I need. I knew that he fooled around before we were married, but he promised that all that was over when he fell in love with me. How could I have been such a fool? Once you're gay you are always gay."

She began to cry. Her tears rolled down her face. Bella cried. He grabbed tissues from his desk and gave them the her. She wiped her eyes. He could see the pain and anguish in her eyes. He felt for her. This was a wretched situation for Jon, he knew, but could not share the truth with her. Jon put his arm around her shoulder to comfort her. He stood next to her with compassion for her and her children.

"I'm sorry, Bella is there anything I can do to help?" he asked out of genuine concern.

"Are you having an affair with my husband?" Bella questioned worthlessly.

"Bella, I am not having an affair with your husband. I'm not exactly sure how he got my card."

"It doesn't matter. If he is fucking anyone, man or woman, our marriage is over. I can't put my self through this kind of hell, again," she assured Jon.

"Bella, you have two children to worry about. I think you need to sit down with your husband and discuss this matter with him immediately. Don't put it off. Excuse me, but did you say again?" Jon inquired.

"Well . . . yeah, once about three years ago, I caught Bruce in bed with another man. I packed his bags and put him out. Then I found out I was pregnant with our third child. Needless to say, he didn't stay away long, maybe a month. So we were back together and putting our marriage back on track with the aid of a marriage counselor and our minister. We were working hard at the marriage, then I suffered a miscarriage. After that, I felt I needed him and didn't want him to leave. He promised that part of his life was over and we would move ahead with life as we'd planned. Then about a year ago, he started going out. Initially, I encouraged him to take some time for himself, he'd go out about once a month. It evolved into a weekly event and then sometimes twice a week. But, I never said anything, I didn't want to push him away. My children needed a strong family unit, especially since we don't have family in the area," she confided.

"You have two children to worry about. You owe it to yourself and your family to at least sit with your husband and discuss your family. Because it is not just the two of you, this involves your children as well. I can make that referral if you need me to."

She said, "I'll need to speak with Bruce before I make an appointment for us. But I know that we need to get this out in the open, once and for all."

Jon said, "After you've spoken with your husband, give me a call to set up the appointment."

"Well, like I said, I'll have to speak with Bruce first, but I know that I have to do something."

She gathered her things to leave Jon's office. She declared, "I've got to do something."

Jon said, concerned, "You still have time left."

"I know, I need to leave. I have taken up enough of your time with my problems. Thank you for listening and your concern."

"Bella, take care of yourself and let me know if I need to make that referral?"

"Thank you again, Jon. I will get back to you about the referral, if not for both of us maybe just for me. I think I might need someone to talk to."

"Please talk to your husband to find the answers you need."

Jon sat in his office and was glad that he'd never been that cruel to a woman. He knew he was gay and did not feel the necessity to include a woman in his life. Many married gay men fooled around, which put their families in harm's way. Although Jon dated women and was engaged once, he knew that he still wanted to be with men. He ended his engagement because he did not want to put her, his fiance, through any more pain than the breakup would cause.

He did not appreciate the faction of homosexuals that felt the need to get married, but continued to sleep with men. They, in Jon's opinion, were cowards. They were afraid, for whatever reason, to be true to themselves. He knew he could never live his life in a closet of any kind.

The remainder of Jon's afternoon was uneventful, dull. Jon sat in his office, he thought about Bella and Bruce. The more he thought about their situation the angrier he became. Jon experienced the misery of growing up with a cheating parent and how it ruined his childhood. He remembered very clearly.

The sound of screaming voices woke Jon. He laid in his bed and prayed the shouting would stop, it didn't. His parents fought all the time. Jon lived in a war zone. He never knew happiness of family without the yelling and screaming.

Through the years, Jon developed a hardened heart when it came to relationships and displaying his emotions. He didn't believe in fidelity. His view was that everybody cheated and that was the way things were. Living in that household nurtured Jon's detached demeanor with his emotions. He did not want children to grow up in a household where there was strife. He lived that life and was detached from emotion because of it.

Jon went down the hall to the rest room, made sure he was alone, closed the stall door and used cocaine. He left the rest room and went back to his office. His last appointment of the day was cut short his client had a family emergency. In his chair, he closed the client's file and leaned back to take a breather.

He felt mucous trickle from his nose. Wiping away the mucous, he looked at the tissue and blood. He blew his nose several times and raced down the hall to the bathroom. He put water up his nose to stop the bleeding. He blew his nose again and it was mucous, only. He looked at himself in the mirror and chanted his mantra, "this is no way to live, I need to make a change."

Back in his office, Jon sat and studied Bella's file. There was only a half a page of case notes, but he labored over them like a novel. He had the file in his hands, but his mind was on his fucked up life. Blood on his tissue was a wake up call, but he didn't listen.

He turn his attention to Bella, Bruce and Cyril. He was in a quandary over this situation. He needed to talk with Cyril. He needed to express how unfair his relationship with Bruce was. Jon needed a game plan so he decided to call Cyril to make a date for drinks, dinner and a movie. He called Cyril.

"Talk to me!" Cyril said.

"Cyril, how are you doing, bitch?" Jon teased.

"Fine slut. How the hell are you?"

"What do you have planned for tonight?"

"What do you have in mind?"

"I was just thinking, we haven't spent anytime together lately. I wanted to know if you wanted to have drinks, dinner and a movie?"

"What gives, Jon? You're usually on a mission, huntin' for a new piece. Why do you want to hang out on a Monday, of all nights?"

"This is my way of apologizing for Sunday. I was out of line and I want to make amends. Because you are my best friend and I know that I hurt you yesterday. I just want to say I'm sorry."

"Well, should I give Bruce a call? He might can get away tonight?"

"No, I would prefer it to be the two of us, so we can chit chat with each other. If Bruce is with us you won't talk to me most of the night, you will be all up in his face. I really want us to hang out and have some fun. Is that too much to ask?"

"He ain't got to come."

"Good, and I don't mean that in a bad way. I want to hang with you."

"Jon, I know something's up? But, I'll play along."

"Anything in a particular you want to see or do you want to go with the flow?"

"There is nothing I'm just dying to see, so let's go with the flow."

"Good, I'll call you when I get home, all right?"

"Don't play wit me, boy? Don't have me come over to your house to kick off in yo' ass. You better call me as soon as you walk in the door."

"As soon as I walk in the door I will call you, all right."

"I will wait for your call."

Jon said, "I'll talk at you then, bye!"

Jon put the receiver on the cradle. He placed Bella's file in his out basket. Her sessions would need to be handled by another therapist. He pondered his evening with Cyril. Would he get through to him that his relationship with a married man was wrong? He could already hear Cyril's response that he is not cheating on anyone. He is not the one doing anything wrong. The evening would prove a test of their friendship.

"Do you need me for anything else?" Claire asked.

"No. Thank you though, have a good evening."

"You too, see you in the a.m..."

"See ya,"

Jon made it home and went straight to the kitchen. He removed the small plate and made a cocktail. He did not call

Cyril. He'd forgotten about their plans. He finished his Tanqueray on the rocks with lime. He called Cyril. They planned to meet at Rossi's, on Orange Blossom Trail, at seven that evening. Jon was trying to come up with a device to discuss Bruce and his wife without being obvious that he knew more about the relationship than Cyril shared.

Jon walked into Rossi's. Cyril sat in a booth across from the entrance. He waved when he saw Jon standing at the door, to invite him over. Jon joined Cyril in the booth. Cyril had a drink and said,

"I've already ordered you a Tanqueray on the rocks with lime." Cyril looked at Jon and wondered what was this evening all about, because he knew Jon well enough to know that something was up. He didn't know what, but he knew that the evening would be quite revealing. Jon asked,

"What's up my friend?" in a Bela Logosi voice.

"You tell me. Now, I know you don't want me to put on my red nose and floppy shoes, so let's have it."

"Heavens no, please don't clown. I just wanted to spend some time with you, as I stated this afternoon. Does there have to be an ulterior motive?"

"No, there does not have to be an ulterior motive, but I know yo' ass and if you coughing up coins for drinks, dinner and a movie, baby, something big is up. Now, you done won the lottery or something and ain't told me? I'll play for a little while, but I am not the one."

"Let's just drink and have dinner. We will talk later this evening. Alrighty, then."

"Thank God! At least now you are admitting that there is something to talk about. Let's get that out of the way first and then get on without evening. Because I have something that I need to discuss with you anyway. Okay, spit it out, bitch."

"What do you need to discuss with me? I ain't got no money to loan, so don't ask. What's up?"

"Remember yesterday?" Cyril asked seriously.

"Sunday, yes I do seem to recall that day," teased Jon.

"Come on be serious, I really need to talk about yesterday," implored Cyril.

"Okay, you make this seem pretty serious. Talk to me."

"Well, yesterday after brunch, Bruce and I went back to my place to do the nasty."

"You always got to have some dick-a-lang. You need to restrict yo' fast ass," Jon interrupted.

"I agree I do need to slow my ass down. Let me tell you about after we made love."

"What happened? You are agreeing with me that you need to slow down. Who are you and what have you done with my best friend, Cyril?"

"Jon, I'm serious."

"I can tell. Okay, what happened after you and Bruce had sex, oh I mean made l–o–v–e–?"

"Jon please. We had a long heart to heart talk. I mean, we really talked about everything and I mean every t'ing." Cyril teased seriously.

"What everything?"

"Jon, he told me he loved me and wanted to be with only me." Looking at Cyril, Jon asked, "and what does Mrs. Bruce have to say about this tidbit of information?"

"Jon do you remember a few years ago, what I was going through. I didn't want to talk to anyone or go out or anything. Do you recall that period?"

"Yeah, I remember you were being a real bitch to everybody even me. You had all the children asking me, what's wrong with Ms. Cyril? Thing, is going through. Oh, yes I recall that time very vividly. You even threw me shade. So, I knew that whatever you were going through, you didn't need my help because you know I am only a phone call away," Jon said sincerely.

"Well, let me tell you what happened."

Jon's mind wandered back to his session with Bella. He tried to put two and two together to come up with four. He thought, Bella told Bruce of her suspicions, she knows he is gay and that he had a boyfriend. Poor Jon sat there dumbfounded, all of his scenarios ended in total disaster for Bella, Bruce and Cyril.

Bruce called Cyril and asked him to come to his house, he had a present for him. He pondered whether he should go the home of a married man, even if his wife was away. After, his split second of pondering Cyril was out of the house in record time, making his way to Bruce's home. Cyril arrived and Bruce invited him into his home.

Cyril admired the decorations and the color scheme of the house and complimented the interior designers for their attention to detail and style. Bruce informed Cyril that his wife was responsible for the opulence of their home. Bruce decided to give Cyril the grand tour, so he would not leave so quickly. They toured each and every room in the house. Cyril was leaving when Bruce pulled him into his arms and kissed him. Cyril was totally taken aback.

They kissed in the home Bruce shared with his wife and two children. Cyril felt their actions were disrespectful, but he wanted Bruce. His hands were all over Cyril, touching, caressing and squeezing. He melted into Bruce's embrace. His lips were soft and gentle to the touch when he opened the receive Bruce's kiss. They made their was to master bedroom. They touched, kissed and made love. They slept naked.

Cyril laid in his arms while they slept. The master bedroom door opened startling Bruce and Cyril. They both jumped from the bed. Bruce's wife stood in the doorway. She closed the door and walked back into the living room. She sat on the sofa. Bruce grabbed his pants and tore out of the bedroom and into the living room.

"Baby. Baby. I can explain. I'm sorry. Honey, I'm so sorry. I thought you were still out of town? You weren't due back until

Wednesday. Baby, I can explain everything." Bruce said.

"What the hell's going on here! Who the fuck is that in my bedroom, in my motherfucking bed? You have lost your ever loving mind, you stupid son-of-a-bitch! So you are some fucking faggot? I don't believe this shit. This bastard is fucking another man! You fucking a man! Oh! My God I married a faggot! Oh, shit! Oh, shit, I probably done got AIDS from this stupid, ignorant, son-of-a-bitch, fucking asshole, motherfucker! You need to pack your shit and get the fuck out!" she screamed and hit Bruce on his chest hard.

"Baby I'm sorry, but I can explain. I... um...ugh. Baby, please don't make me leave, I need you and our children to make my life complete. You are my world! I love you more than life itself! You are all that matters to me! Please don't make me leave, I need you! I need you!" Bruce cried as he fell to his knees. "I'm begging you please don't make me leave. I'll do anything, anything at all, please don't make me leave. I need you! I love you and I need to bvee with my kids!" he cried as tears streamed down his face.

"You might as well get up and go pack your bags, you got to go! What were you thinking, I could have had the kids with me! You laying up in the bed naked with a man! How could I explain that to them! Get out of my sight and get out of this house! You make me sick. You're a pathetic piece of shit. Just go!" she yelled.

Cyril came out of the bedroom, and walked through the living room toward the door. He told Mrs. Toussaint, "I'm sorry. I don't know what came over me. I apologize for disrespecting you and your home, Mrs. Toussaint. I'll be leaving now," Cyril said sadly.

Throwing one small statue and then another at Cyril she screamed, "Get out of my house you faggot. Just get your faggot ass out of my house." She yelled, "Get out, faggot. Get out, faggot."

"Child, I ran out the damn house and never looked back. I got my ass in my car and hit it. That was one of the worst thing I think I've ever done." Cyril said.

"No, the worst thing you ever done was to keep seeing him after you knew he was married. That is the worst thing you've ever done. You knew he had a wife and children, but you put your desire ahead of his family. Why?" he paused. "Why, did you feel the necessity to disrupt someone's life. That is the worst thing you've ever done. You know I love you, but that was really low."

"No, I didn't keep seeing him. All that drama happened about three years ago. You are right that was scandalous. I didn't see Bruce after that, until about year ago. Then we started talking and we would get together about once a month, in the beginning. Then Bruce said he could get away about once a week and then sometimes more. So we've been kicking since then."

"I wish you could find someone single and leave that woman's husband alone. I love and only want he best for you. So, you better wash that man right out of your hair, you better wash that man right out of your hair," Jon sang.

"When you're right you're right. I will do just that. Remember, I told you I needed to talk with you well, Bruce and I had a very interesting conversation. He told that he loves me and wants to leave his wife and kids, so we can be together. I was floored. I looked at him and saw that he was sincere. I was flabbergasted. Then it occurred to that if he found it that easy to walk away from a wife and children, then he was not really ready for a committed relationship. Especially a gay relationship with me!"

Jon looked in amazement at Cyril. He said through mock crying, "my baby boy is growing up. It is such a wonderful feeling to see your boy grow into a man." Jon stopped teasing Cyril, "I have been trying to tell you the same things for a long time now. Why have you finally listened to what I have been telling you all along?"

"That's just it, I don't know and for the first time in a very long time I really don't care. I think that I love Bruce, I might even be in love with him. But there is a huge problem, his wife. There are also two other little obstacles, his kids. Jon, I don't deserve to be the second anything to anyone. I should be his one and only, if I can't be that, I don't want anything from him." Cyril said solemnly.

That was the first time Cyril ever admitted he wanted and needed more from a relationship than just sex. He had come to realize that there was more to a relationship. He had known it all along but chose not to adhere to his conscience. He was now on a plane that could take him many places emotionally. Cyril now wanted more from people, because he expected more from himself. Jon's words at brunch had a profound impact on Cyril and he would forever be grateful.

"I think that everything with Bruce is over. I told him yesterday I did not want anything to do with him. Then I asked him to leave. It was very difficult, but I told him to go and I stayed in last night to do a little introspection. See, I do listen to you. I don't always tell you that I tried some techniques that you taught me. Because yo' head is big enough as it is."

"My head, big. I know you didn't go there. Don't have me clown up in here! I hope that it is over with Bruce, that's what I wanted to talk to about tonight. You beat me to the punch. I am pleased. Let me make a toast. To my best friend in the world I pray that we will always be friends and be there for each other, I love you and hope that our friendship will last until the end of time." Jon said as they clinked their glasses.

"Jon, thank you for being my friend. I know I don't always act like it, but I do love you and I am blessed that you are my best friend."

"Now that we got your love out of the way. I want to talk to you about mine." Jon confessed.

"Not Mr. love'em and leave'em, not the notorious Knight. You have a love life. I thought that you only had fuck buddies? You mean that little Puerto Rican has pierced that glacier you call a heart? I don't believe it," Cyril teased.

" Look, I've listened to you and all your drama. So, please return the favor and don't treat me so harshly. You know I'm fragile," mocked Jon.

"Come on, Cyril, I'm serious."

"I'm all ears. So, talk."

"Contrary to popular belief, it is not the little Puerto Rican boy, he's back in Brooklyn. I'm talking about somebody right here in Gotham City. Remember, yesterday at brunch?"

"Sunday, oh yeah, I remember yesterday," Cyril teased.

"Hardy har har, that was so funny I forgot to laugh. Okay, listen. Remember the bartender at the cafe. His name is Ian."

Cyril interrupted Jon, "Not the bartender? Can't you go anywhere without picking up some damn body? You turn Sunday Brunch into a quest for sex."

"Believe me, its not like that at all. Have you ever met someone, when you met you had all these things in common and there's a chemistry? You just clicked from the very beginning? Well, that's kind of what happened yesterday with Ian and me. After you guys left yesterday I went to the bar for another mimosa and struck up a conversation with the bartender. We started talking and before I knew it I had invited him to my place last night for drinks. I didn't know if he was gay, straight, bi or what and it didn't matter. I just wanted to be in his presence."

Cyril looked at Jon. "To quote you, who are you and where the hell is my best friend, Jon."

"Listen I didn't care I wanted to be near him. So he came over last night and we talk, listened to music. I finally found someone that appreciates my musical tastes. Ian loved my apartment and how it's decorated. We talked about art, artists and local galleries. Oh my God we had a wonderful evening.

Then it happened, we embrace, fireworks! We only hugged each other and there was a connection, chemistry. Ian was so taken with our touch that when he went to the kitchen to get our drinks, he forgot what he went to the kitchen for. I mean it was incredible. Cyril, you've never heard me talk like this about anybody. Our chemistry was electrical. When I looked into his eyes after the embrace I think I fell in love. Love at first sight and all, I know. There is something so powerful between us that I've had Ian on the brain all day long."

"Damn, Juan hasn't been gone for a full twenty-four hours yet. Look at you, done went and fell in love with somebody else. I just don't understand you and your fickle ass. Look, what about Juan, Ernest or a half dozen other I could name. What makes Ian different?"

"I can see a future with Ian. A long term relationship. I can see us living together. I can take him to meet the folks. I might even consider...penetration...na. He has mesmerized me and I don't know what to do. Well there is one tiny detail, he has a lover. I don't know how long they been together and I don't care. I want him," Jon said urgently.

"Jon didn't we learn anything from my experience with Bruce?" Cyril asked slowly.

"This is not the same, there are no children involved."

"No. No children just a lover, but what the hell, who cares Ian has a lover," Cyril said candidly.

"This is different. He is my soul mate. We were pure magic. We didn't make love we became love. Our bodies melded, we were one. I feel it and I know he does, too."

"You are seriously deranged and delusional. Jon, you met him yesterday. You have not known him for twenty-four hours. There is no way you are in love. Look, you don't even know him."

"Say what you must, you didn't feel it. I know you have never experienced real love before, so you would not understand."

"Look, don't take me there," Cyril warned.

"I didn't mean that the way it came out. I am crazy for this man and I don't know why? It is scary and exciting. I hope he calls me tonight. Damn! listen to me, I sound like a lovesick little bitch. I told myself earlier today I was putting Ian out of my mind. I need to check myself. This is getting a little out of control. Forget a movie, I need to go the PH. I need to find a hot little boy to satisfy me tonight, to get Ian out of my head."

"Okay, mister mister. As soon as we're done with dinner, you're off to PH and I's going home,"

"I need your support. You know how I get when I'm on a mission. I just need a diversion."

"You need to take your ass home, so you can get up and go to work tomorrow, on time."

"Can't you see I'm in pain?" Jon questioned.

"Like I said you need to take your ass home and get some rest."

"You are right. I will go home and take my ass to bed."

After dinner the Cyril and Jon moved to the bar. They had a few more cocktail and flirted with their waitress, Leslie. They had done a great deal of talking. Both had agendas to make changes in their lives, starting Tuesday. Jon was to stop thinking about Ian and get on with his life. Cyril was to move on without Bruce.

Jon made it home and was in the kitchen with the small plate. He emptied the last contents of the bag on the plate, but decided to rebag it for tomorrow morning. He poured himself another cocktail and went into the living room. The soothing sounds of Diana Ross engulfed the room and washed over Jon in his black silk boxers. He was assessing his conversation with Cyril and mentally preparing for bed.

He was on the verge of sleep when the phone rang and interrupted him. Jon decided to answer, Cyril might need an ear. He answered the call; it was Juan.

"Hi, baby!" Juan exclaimed.

74

"Hey, what's up?" Jon asked.

"That's what I should be asking you. I called yesterday and left a message. You didn't call me
back. What's up with that?"

"Just busy."

"So, do you miss me?"

"Of course. I don't know how I got to bed last night without you in my arms." Jon said making faces, lying.

"Are you okay, you sound a little distracted? Did I catch you at a bad time? Do you have . . . company? What's up?" Juan questioned.

"Look, nothing's up. So, how was first day back in the Big Apple? Do you miss me?" Jon said knowing this would endear him to Juan.

"You know I miss you. I've left messages saying I miss you. Back in Brooklyn, same as I left it. Nothings changed. Except that I miss you. I know we are only friends and I will not be calling all the time to make you not want to talk to me. Please indulge me this one time. Believe me it won't happen again. Believe that."

"Hey, just like we said before you left, you got some dick. We ain't trying be lovers or anything, but when I'm in NYC or when you're in O-town we can git wit it. Right! That is what we said. No, I don't have a problem with you calling."

"I just don't want any drama for your mama about me calling you. Because like I said you sound a bit distracted tonight. So, just wanted to say hello and let you know that you are missed." Juan said as he hung the phone.

Jon returned to the sofa and turned Ms. Ross up. He finished his cocktail and decided not to have another. He turned off the stereo and lights in the living room and went to his bedroom. Checking to make sure the alarm was set, he reach over and pick up the last month's Ebony. When he reached for the magazine his nostrils were permeated with Ian's scent, he threw the pillow across the room. He thumbed through and found a

75

article that he'd started and didn't finish. Ian entered his thoughts, yet again. Jon was determined to get him out of his mind. The article was not enough to keep his mind off of Ian. He fell asleep with thoughts of Ian drifting in his head.

Tuesday, August 9, 1988

The radio blasted like thunderous rain during a hurricane. Jon jolted in the bed.He turned down the volume and laid back for few more minutes of relaxation. The cool jazz gently eased him completely awake. The music made him want to wear something dark, very noir. He thought he would wear his charcoal grey double breasted suit with his black , charcoal and white tie. That suit made him feel very urbane.

Today would be a day from hell. Jon made his way to the shower. After his shower, Jon went to the kitchen, made coffee and used the small plate. The coffee brewed and he sniffed. Jon sniffed half the contents in the bag and put it in his pocket for later. He finished dressing and was out the door in a flash. He was wired more than usual from a line of cocaine. He didn't think twice about it and was en route to work.

Jon arrived at the office on time and ready to work. Claire was not at her desk. Jon flipped through his day planner and noted a meeting with the executive director. He would deal with that in the afternoon. Isabella Toussaint's file was in his out basket. He completed transferring the case and put the file away. He thought he should give her a call to determine if he needed to make a referral. He called.

He phoned Mrs. Toussaint, "Good morning Bella, this is Jon from the help group."

"Good morning Jon, how are you?" Bella asked.

"A better question is how are you today?"

"Fair to middling. I have had better days," she shared.

"I can understand. Is there anything I can do for you?"

"No, but thanks for your concern."

"I was calling to check with you concerning the referral. I still have your file open, pending a referral. What's my next step?"

"Oh, I don't know. Bruce got in late last night and up early this morning, I have not had a chance to talk with him yet."

"I'll keep the file open pending a referral until I hear from you? Is that fine with you?"

"That sounds like a plan. Keep it open. Like I told you yesterday, if he doesn't what to come in I might come alone to talk. But, if I come alone I want to talk with you and no one else. Can that be arranged?"

"That should not be a problem. If there is a problem I will call to make the referral. How's that?"

"Jon, if I can't work with you I won't come back to the help group. Is that understood?"

"I understand, but there are times when extenuating circumstance prohibit us from treating certain clients," Jon said.

"Will there be extenuating circumstances with me?" Bella inquired.

"None that I see at present," Jon lied.

"Good, keep my file open. As soon as I talk with Bruce, I will give you a call. Thanks Jon, I appreciate your concern, good bye," Bella said before she hung up the phone.

Jon put the reciever on the cradle. He knew he could not treat Bella it was conflict of interest. If it were ever found out that he knew his client's husband, he would be in deep trouble. He hoped that Cyril would keep his vow and not see Bruce anymore. That would help, but it would still not be ethical for Jon to treat Bella.

Claire informed Jon that his two morning clients cancelled. Jon had the rest of the morning to conduct some introspection. He knew he would not like what lurked inside, but he knew it was time.

He buzzed Claire to tell her, "please take messages the rest of the morning. I don't want to be disturbed. Thank you."

Jon knew what he needed to do, but opted to skim the surface instead of delving deeper into his psyche to unravel the truth behind his emotional detachment. He wondered how could he be so void of emotion when so many people around him constantly showed him emotional stability.

Unfortunately, none of his emotional learning was done at home. Home was a place of conflict and turmoil. At home Jon learned how a relationship should not be conducted. There was always a source of contention. His parents publicly loved each other, but behind closed doors was where the truth lay.

Mother and father were not exactly like Cliff and Claire Huxtable. They were never on one accord. They were always at odds with one another. She gave him too much attention. He spent too much time at work. It was constantly a battle for time and blame. They both got their fair share of both. Jon was the one that suffered

His relationship role models were both devoid of any type of affection. He did not know that it was fine for him to hug and kiss his father, as he did his mother. There was no affection shown in the home. The only affection he knew that his parents shared was sex. So sex became a source of affection, not affection, but power for Jon.

Sex was his source of affection, the more sex he had the more powerful he felt. He deemed himself the object of desire. Others would have to cater to his sexual appetite. Because he was an attractive man, many women and men succumbed to his charms. His reputation, Notorious Knight, was well earned. Something he was not necessarily proud of, but it was a part of what made him Jon Knight.

Claire buzzed Jon to tell him, "Jon, its lunch time and I'm leaving my desk. Do you need anything while I'm out?"

He came out of deep thought to respond, "no, thank you I'm fine."

He decided to have lunch at *the cafe*. Jon closed his files and left the office. At *the cafe*, to his surprise was Ian sitting with an elderly looking man. Jon did not acknowledge Ian, fearing that elderly man was his lover, Enrique. He sat at a table alone. The waiter took his order. He had a glass of zinfandel while he waited for his lunch. He felt an emotional tidal wave every time he looked at Ian. He tortured himself for the duration of his lunch. He mouthed, "call me," to Ian before he left "the cafe" for the office.

Jon reviewed and transferred case notes from his pad to the files. He knew he had a meeting with Mr. Hamilton, but he took a break from his files. A line of coke was what he needed at this very moment. Jon checked his pocket and made sure the bag was still there. He went down the hall to the rest room. He check the stalls to make sure he was alone. Closing the stall door for privacy, he sniffed his last line of coke. To the sink for water and he went back to his office.

Claire buzzed Jon to tell him, "Jon, Mr. Hamilton is ready for you now."

"Thank you Claire, let him know I'll right in. You know I hate these meetings with Hamilton."

DETACHED

"I know." Claire said.

"So, why do you make me go to them? Huh!" Jon teased.

"Don't go, but I'll need to find another therapist to work with because I need my pennies," Claire joked.

"Girl, I need my coins, too. So I better get on up in this meetin' fo' Hamilton send his posse fo' me," Jon joked.

He hated these meetings with Hamilton. Jon would get worked up because he had to defend his decisions with different clients. He put on his poker face to battle with Hamilton. When he arrived at Hamilton's office his assistant told him, "take a seat, Mr. Hamilton will be with you in a moment. He's on a call."

Jon knew the game all too well. Hamilton would make you sit out here for a few minutes to get you just a bit irritated before he'd meet with you. Once he had you where he wanted you, he thought he had the advantage. Jon was one step ahead of him this time. He told Hamilton's assistant, "tell him I'll be back in about five minutes to give him time to finish his call. I'll have Claire buzz before I come over."

Hamilton's assistant looked at Jon as he walked out of the office and down the hall. He refused to play Hamilton's game today. He stepped into his office, Claire gave him a puzzled look. Jon stood there for a minute to wait for Hamilton's assistant to call. Claire did not know what to make of his appearance because he was supposed to be in a meeting with Mr. Hamilton. Jon went into his office and waited.

After about ten minutes Jon told Claire, "let Hamilton's assistant know that I am on my way and to please let me know if there will be any delays." He leaned back in chair and waited another five minutes before he left his office. As Jon left his office he told Claire, "please buzz me in Hamilton's office in about fifteen minutes if I'm not back. There is an emergency with a client and I'm desperately needed."

"Sure thing, Mr. Knight," Claire said.

"Hey, what's with Mr. Knight?"

"I may need to get in practice of using Mr. or Ms. who-ever. You gonna cross Mr. Hamilton once too often," Claire said concerned.

"I know, I know."

Jon entered the office and Hamilton's assistant told Jon, "take a seat. Mr. Hamilton will be with in a moment. He's on a call."

"Tell Mr. Hamilton when he has time for our meeting I will be at his disposal. Please buzz Claire when he is ready for me, thank you," Jon said sternly. He turned to leave.

"He just finished his call. You can go in now," Mr. Hamilton's assistant said.

Jon entered the abyss to face the cantankerous Mephistopheles. Like many before, Jon, him went to plead his case. He took a seat. Mr. Hamilton's assistant buzzed him with a call he had to take. He took the call.

"I don't give a damn about the other fathers. I can't make the meeting on Friday night, I'm flying to Chicago for a confer-ence. I told you that two weeks ago. I can't make it and that is that. I'll talk with you when I get home," he said and slammed the phone down. "It's always something when you have kids." he said to Jon.

"You don't have any kids, do you?"

"No, I don't," he responded.

"Well, let's get down to it. I reviewed your special pro-ject request to implement a counseling program in the Ivy Lane area. What made you want to go into that neighborhood?" Mr. Hamilton asked with a discerning tone in his voice.

"The idea generated from a conversation I had with a kid at career day in the neighborhood. As, I talked with him I realized that he and other kids might need someone to talk to. I planned to set everything like a rap session. Where there is no pressure for them to talk if they don't want to, but the I will include incentives for the kids that participate the most. In the end all the kids will be taken to Disney or a Magic game. However, during the sessions kids will receive little educational tools like pens, notebooks, pads, cassettes and other items I've gotten donated."

"How much time are you requesting? How will it effect your regular caseload? Will you still be available for new clients?"

Jon looked relieved. "I'm only requesting twenty hours a month for the next nine months. I need to have in-kind services from various agencies to get the program off the ground. The rap sessions are Saturday. The twenty hours will be one hour a day for administrative and one-on-one sessions with kids and their parents. Hopefully, our program will succeed in helping kids deal with the pressures of growing up in a neighborhood where the most respected people are drug dealers."

"Jon I am impressed. I read the proposal and thought it was a well-planned project. Listening to your enthusiasm, I will help in any way I can. If you need any office supplies, administrative services or anything, just let me know." Mr. Hamilton said.

"Thank you Mr. Hamilton. I appreciate your generosity. I will make a list of supplies we need and ask Claire, my assistant, to help, also. Once again, thank you, Mr. Hamilton, I really appreciate your support," Jon exclaimed.

"You are welcome and Jon when we are alone, call me Hamilton," he laughed.

Embarrassed, Jon shook Mr. Hamilton's hand, thanked him again and left his office. He walked down the hall on a cloud of air. He was so high with pure excitement about his project that nothing could phase him now. Jon rounded the corner to his office, smiling.

Looking up from some file Claire asked, "what happened?"

"Remember the Ivy Lane Project? Mr. Hamilton approved it and told me that any assistance I needed he would provide. I can't believe it. Now I feel guilty about how I'm always talking badly about, him. But I'm glad he came through for my project." Jon said.

"I'm so glad he approved the project. It is a worthwhile venture for those kids. I hope it all goes well."

"Oh, you'll know first hand. He told me that could have some administrative assistance with this project. Hello, administrative assistance," Jon informed Claire. He leaned over her desk and whispered, "You can take off an hour early every day for the next nine months. Now, ain't I a good boss?" Jon inquired.

"You are the best."

"I won't need any help until late November-early December to prepare some reports to the housing authority. I mean unless you just want to come down sometime. Seriously, late November early December, so don't get too accustomed to the short work week," Jon teased

"I won't. Thanks Jon I really appreciate you and what you are trying to do for the kids."

Jon was very excited about his meeting with Mr. Hamilton, he needed to share. Jon made a few phone calls to his Ivy Lane Project Committee. He felt mucous drip from his nose. He wiped his nose, blood was on the tissue. That reminded him he needed to call Eric. Eric did not answer. He called Cyril to find out how his first day without Bruce went. Cyril was not in the office. He pulled out some files to review. The rest of his afternoon was open, his two appointments canceled.

Jon stayed in his office the rest of the afternoon and thought about life and how his was fucked up. He thought, *I should return to introspection and life with mother and father.* He decided that he wanted a distraction instead. Seeing Ian at lunch did not help with his obsession. Jon's mind traced the hairs around Ian's mouth. He could almost feel Ian's body, the memory was so commanding. Refusing rapture with Ian, Jon decided to get out the office and

take a drive or go catch a movie or go to an art gallery.

The art gallery was a perfect distraction for Jon, a place where he could get lost and still open his mind to new perspectives. Jon took the scenic route to the gallery. He drove past

Lake Ivanhoe and Lake Eola. Downtown he past Cyril's office building and Jon started to check to see if he was in the office, but thought not. This was Jon time and he didn't need anyone to interfere. He wandered around the gallery admiring sculptures from New Guinea and Ghana. He was fascinated with African Art and culture, although he never studied. Jon like many people enjoyed viewing the art and feeling a connection to mother Africa, but never did anything to understand the people, culture or history of the continent, apathetic.

Jon purchased a hand beaded necklace and bracelet imported from Ghana. He loved the detailing of the bone craved cylinder with the onyx stone center. He put on his new acquisitions and left the gallery. These would be added to his African jewelry collection. He'd purchased many other pieces from the gallery.

Jon left the gallery and headed for the nearest happy hour. He was a few blocks away from the Parliament House so he thought, "what the hell." He turned in the direction of the PH and was on his way. PH was usually slow in the early evening late afternoon, but today could prove to be different.

Before he got to the Parliament House, Jon saw an attractive man pass him on Orange Blossom Trail. He thought, "should I see were he goes?" Jon tapped the steering wheel and made a turn in pursuit of the cutie in the car. He sped up to drive beside the good looking black man. Once he was next to the blue BMW, he made the obligatory eye contact. He looked back at Jon and smiled. Jon thought, that's a good sign. Now, I'll look again and see what he does. He loved this cat and mouse, flirting with total strangers. For Jon, it was a definitive rush. The BMW pulled into the bookstore parking lot. Jon turned in after him. He went inside as did Jon. Inside they looked at each other seductively. He looked at Jon before he left the bookstore, Jon looked and followed.

He got into his BMW and pulled out the parking lot. Jon was still in pursuit. The BMW drove down the trail a few miles and turned into an apartment complex. Jon drove a few car lengths behind him and made the turn, also. Jon traced his pattern and parked his car two spaces from the BMW. Cutie went upstairs and opened the first apartment door on the left, leaving the door partly open. Jon thought,"I'll go inside to see what happens."

Jon pushed the door slightly and entered the apartment. He stood there near the door.

Cutie extended his hand. "Hi, I'm Lamar. Come on in, the water's fine."

"I'm Jon" he said shaking Cutie's hand.

"So, what's up?"

"Well, I don't know you tell me."

"I noticed you followed me home. Thank you for making sure I got home safely. Now, is there anything I can do you for?" Lamar asked seductively.

"It depends on you. Do you mind if I get more comfortable?"

"Keep doing what you were doing before, follow me."

"Right behind you."

"And that's where I want you, too."

"Works for me."

Jon followed Lamar into his bedroom. The room was tastefully decorated in contemporary styles, in black and white. They kissed. They had raw unadulterated sex. More alcohol. No coke.

Jon was on his way home after his afternoon of diversions. Now he could focus on the rest of his day and celebrate his triumph with the Ivy Lane Project. When he got home he checked his messages. Cyril, Eric, Juan and a Ivy Lane Project colleague called, but no message from Ian. This made him distraught, but he had made a pact with himself that he would put Ian out of his mind. As hard as he tried he could not. He called the cafe, but Ian was not there. He called Eric.

"Yo, man what's up?" Jon asked.

"Chillin' in the cut. What do you need my friend?" Eric

mocked in a ghoulish tone.

"What are you holding?"

"Hold up my brotha, I'll be over in a few. Peace out." Eric said before he put the phone on the cradle.

"Cool, I'll be waiting."

Jon opened mail and prepared to pay bills. He sat at his desk and began to write checks. He called Cyril and continued writing checks.

"Hello," Cyril said sluggishly.

"Well, hello to you, too," Jon said. "How are you doing today. You sound awful. What's up?"

"I didn't sleep well last night. I tossed and turned all night. I don't know what's wrong. All I know is that today has been a bear. I am glad it is over. What are you getting into to night?"

"Does not seeing Bruce anymore have anything to do with your restless night?" Jon teased.

"Not at all. Thank you very much. Now what are you doing tonight?"

"Eric is on his way over and after he leaves, I don't know."

"Talking about living without something. I am not the one for that foolishness."

Trying to convince Cyril and himself . Jon said,"It is not a habit, just a diversion. I can stop. Anytime I want. I haven't chosen to stop yet. I only do it on the weekends and during the evenings. Not every day, either."

"Yeah, keep telling yourself that until they cart your ass off to Charter," Cyril said out of concern.

"They will not cart me off to Charter, thank you very much. I'd just continue to go to work every day and meet with an in-house therapist. So I wouldn't be going to Charter. Thank you very much,"Jon joked.

"You think you have all the answers, don't you? Just remember when you're going to work and seeing a therapist about your problem. Oh, but it is not a habit, you can quit any-time you want. You just haven't chosen to quit yet!" mocked Cyril.

"Look I understand your concern, but I have everything under control. I didn't get a chance to tell you my good news. Its about my Ivy Lane Project."

Laughing as he spoke, "Jon, I don't believe you. You are looking to help the kids deal with their drug infested neigh-borhoods, but you are a part of the problem. You keep the drug dealers in business."

"Ha! Ha! Ha! Very funny mother fucker. That shit ain't funny. I think that I can do some good for the kids in the neighborhood. I know I am playing things a little close, but I know what I need to do."

"I hope all goes well with the project for the kids sake. I know what it is a needed service.   And not enough of us are putting back into the black neighborhoods. We get ours and get out. At great deal of us don't look back. We are in pursuit of the almighty dollar and to hell with everything else. I com-mend you for your effort and I pray all goes well for you and the kids. Maybe something will rub off on you. Wouldn't that be a novel idea?"

"Mock me if you will, but I have everything under con-trol. I have my new project and I've cut my work week down by five hours. Time that will be donated to the Ivy Lane Project, so there," Jon taunted.

"Like I said before, I commend you for your efforts. It just seems a bit ironic that you would want to help in the fight against drugs."

"No! No, you are missing the point of the project. The Ivy Lane Project is to help kids in the neighborhood cope with their environment. My project is not a fight against drugs; it's giving kids a better way to cope with their lives."

"I get your point. It is still ironic to me! Now, enough about your pet project. What are you doing tonight after you meet with Eric?"

"I'm open for suggestions. Do you have anything in mind?"

"We didn't catch a flick last night, are you game?"

"Um, a film is not . . . on the top my list. Next idea?"

"Bitch! Don't ask me for a suggestion and then dismiss it. Where do you want to go, its Tuesday night there aren't a lot of choices."

"Let's go to Southern Nights?"

"Cool, are we meeting? Are you picking me up? Am I picking you up? How do you want to work it?"

"Okay, let's meet so you can leave whenever?"

"What time?"

"Eleven. That gives me time to get a shower and catch up on a little reading. I'll meet you out front. Okay baby," Jon whispered.

"See you then tramp. Bye."

Jon continued working on his bills. There was a knock at the door. Jon peeked through the peep hole and saw that it was Eric. He opened the door to let Eric in and said, "Come on in, the water's fine." He went to the kitchen and asked Eric, "do you want a cocktail?"

"Now, you know I want a cocktail. I don't even know why you asked?"

Jon brought the drinks to the living room and asked Eric, "what do you have?"

He took a plastic bag from his pocket and placed it on the table then said,"this is what I got. Now what do you got?"

Jon took some money from his pocket, gave it Eric and said,"a few coins."

Eric took the money and put it in his pocket. Jon retrieved the small plate and emptied some of the contents of the plastic bag onto the plate. He cut and chopped the cocaine and formed four hefty lines. He passed the plate to Eric. He took the plate and quickly sniffed the two lines of cocaine. Eric

89

placed the small plate in front of Jon and took a swallow of his drink. Jon picked up the plate and carefully sniffed each line allowing the powder to enter his head. He took a deep breath for maximum cocaine penetration. Eric was at the sink putting water up his nose; Jon followed suit. Jon made more cocktails. They did four more lines of coke and had a few more drinks. After a while Eric left. Jon needed to prepare to meet Cyril at the Southern Nights and he still had to take a shower. More alcohol. More coke.

Jon arrived about ten minutes later than Cyril, who was usually very punctual.   They hugged each other and headed inside to check out the amateur strip contest. The contest was a lot of fun because the contestants were men and women, and the women won a great deal of the time. They would show their tits and the crowd would go crazy. Cyril and Jon got their early enough to get good seats right up front. They ordered cocktails and waited for the show to begin.

"The crowd is not too thick tonight? I wonder is there something else going on in town that I don't know about?" Cyril asked.

"How could their possibly be something else going on that you, Mr. All About Orlando, don't know about? For shame. You are always in the know." Jon teased.

"Well, let me roam around and catch the word. If there is something going on, I will find out tonight," Cyril vowed.

"I'll wait on your party report," Jon said. He observed the crowd looking for a new conquest. There were a lot of pretty boys at the club that night.   Jon wanted to bed down one before the night was over. He looked at various ones and could not decide which he would go after. Someone tapped Jon on the shoulder and he turned to see an attractive black man with blonde hair and grey eyes, not contacts.   He had a tight muscular body and Jon wanted him. They talked for a few minutes until Cyril joined them. Cyril sat on his stool and the blond guy stood between Jon's legs facing Cyril.

"I ain't got no word on anything going on tonight. Maybe the children are tired? I don't know, but I ain't heard nothing." Cyril said upon his return to Jon.

"I heard that a circuit party was happening tonight in Maitland. I think a lot of people are there. I don't do the circuit anymore. I was a circuit queen at one time. Traveling all over to catch the next party wave. Thank God those days are over," said the blond guy.

"Cyril this is . . . a cute black man. I have no idea what his name is?" Jon confessed.

"This is my best friend Cyril and my name is Jon."

"Nice to meet you Cyril, my name is Melvin, but my friends call me Mel." He turn to face Jon and leaned in and whispered, "I know who you are, Notorious Knight."

"Oh, so you know who I am, do you. So, who am I?" Jon questioned.

"You are one of the most respected therapists in Orlando. You have an insatiable sexual appetite. You don't do relationships and I'll be sleeping with you tonight?" Mel said.

"You are right on all counts, especially the last one," Jon conceded.

"Why is that I can't take you nowhere. Every time I take you out the damn house you picking up somebody. What is the deal?" Cyril teased.

"I know, I know, what is a boy to do." Jon joked. The trio laughed, drank and watched the strip contest. After the contest was over Jon, Mel and Cyril danced the rest of the night away. Mel was one of those boys that knew what he wanted and went flat out after it. Mel's demeanor intrigued Jon to the utmost. The evening at Southern Nights was a blast. The DJ announced," Last call! Last Call!" Cyril made his way to the door and waved good bye to Jon and Mel nasty dancing on the floor. They waved and never missed a beat. Jon was glad that he'd met Mel, another diversion.

Jon invited Mel back to his place which seemed strange

because he'd already indicated that he'd be spending the night. A great majority of the guys Jon did, didn't know him or were visitors, like Juan from Brooklyn. Regardless, Jon had a reputation that preceded him. Jon and Mel had more drinks, coke and wild passionate sex. Jon always lived up to or surpassed his reputation. Mel did not spend the night. He left shortly after the sex was over. More alcohol. More coke.

Wednesday, August 10,1988

He lay exhausted from his early morning sexual aerobics. The alarm clock blasted cutting through the tranquility. Jon vaulted from his bed. Jon made his way to the bathroom and relieved himself. He took a long hot shower to wake himself up and get in the work frame of mind.

He made his way to the kitchen, still listless from dancing and sexing all night. He knew what he needed, before his first cup of java. He removed the small plate from the cupboard. Jon made two thick lines and sniffed them one at a time. He leaned against the counter with his head back, to allow the coke to flow freely into his mind. Deep breaths so the coke could pierce his brain. The coke was more absolute than usual and the thick lines took their toll on Jon.

Jon was coked up, so much that his brain was frozen. He sat

at the breakfast nook and drank his coffee. He thought, what will today hold for me, the kid? Only the good Lord knows. I hope that all will go well today and all my appointments are progressive. Jon stood putting his coffee cup in the sink and making his way to the bedroom to get dressed for work. He toured his closet seeking the right combination for today's attitude, which was 'don't fuck with me I have an agenda.' He selected a navy jacket, twill khakis, a powder blue Kenneth Gordon pinpoint oxford shirt and no tie. He dressed listening to the soothing sounds of Anita Baker's *Giving you the best that I got* CD, Jon got dressed and was off to the office. Flying high and on time.

He arrived at the office early so many people were not in yet. In his office Jon sat behind his desk and pulled out some files to get a jump start on his day. Claire peeked her head in his office and asked, "would you like a cup of coffee?"

"No thank you, but I do need your assistance."

"I need to get a cup of joe and I'll be there in a few minutes. Okay, Jon?"

"That will be fine."

Jon needed to discuss the Ivy Lane Project with Claire. They needed to device the plan of attack for the neighborhood. How to approach the parents without being presumptuous, that their children needed psychological help. He did need the parents as allies to win the children over to the program or did he need to recruit the kids first and bring the parents around? That was the situation for which he needed Claire's expertise. He put the files aside, retrieved the Ivy Lane Project file and waited for Claire to return. Then the phone rang; it was Cyril.

"Good morning, who are we today? Did we get enough sleep last night or should I say this morning?" asked Cyril.

"And a good morning to you, too. Yes, I did get enough sleep. Thank you very much. And what else do you want to know? Because you never call me at work this early in the morning.What's up?" he asked.

"Well, I need your advice," Cyril said.

"Let me check my book to set up an appointment," Jon teased.

"Hardy har har. You are not funny. Okay."

"What is the situation and I hope that it does not involve Bruce Toussaint?"

"Sorry, but it does involve Bruce. If you don't want to help I don't have a problem with that," Cyril lied.

"Okay, let's hear it."

"Bruce called me last night. He asked if he could come over to talk. I told him that it was not a good idea. He begged and pleaded and I gave in. So he came over and we just talked, nothing else happened. I vowed that I would not, knowingly, make love to another married man. He shared with me about his wife and their talk about the marriage. He wants to leave his wife and children for me," Cyril said directly.

"What was your response to his request?" Jon asked dreading the answer.

"I told him if he wanted to leave his wife that was fine and dandy, but please don't leave her thinking that you can move in with me and start a new life. I might be falling in love with you, but I will never have another woman's man living with me," Cyril said defiantly.

"Good for you. So far I don't hear a need for advice." questioned Jon.

"I'm getting to that point. Bruce asked if he could stay with me as a friend for a few weeks until he made up his mind about his next step. Should I let him stay?" Cyril asked, knowing the answer to expect from Jon.

"Well Cyril, what do you think? Do you think that living in the same house with
someone that you are falling in love with is a good situation to put yourself in?"

"No, but under the other hand if I want to establish a friendship with him, shouldn't I first be a friend?" Cyril raised the question.

"I understand the fact that you want to be his friend. but try to look at things from a different perspective. Okay, you still have feelings for Bruce, correct?" Jon hypothesized.

"I do have strong feelings for him," Cyril agreed.

"Late one night you both are at home. You have a few glasses of wine or some cocktails. One t'ing leads to another, you wake in bed with each other. You are thinking that this is going to work, we've made love. He's living with me. All is right with the world," Jon points out.

"I can see that happening and that is why he should not stay with me?" Cyril questioned.

"Look, Cyril, if you want to take care of this sorry piece of shit, be my guest. Just make sure you know what you are getting into." Jon said flatly.

"What do you mean?" Cyril asked.

"You will be in the middle of a bitter divorce or is he planning on divorcing his wife? What are his plans for his family? These are the questions that need answers. My advice to you, but I know that you will make up your own mind, is walk away from Bruce and this whole messy situation. Don't get caught in the middle of his marital mess. Because in the end he will be free from his wife and you will have been the transition person that helped him through the maze. Once he is out of the maze of marriage, he will be out of your life, as well. You will be a part of that atrocious circumstance that he wants to put behind him. You will have helped him with everything and he will not be the man that you want in your life. He will move on to someone not included in his baggage," Jon counseled Cyril.

"Do you think that he would leave me after all that we would have gone through?"

"Cyril, he is leaving his wife and two small children. Do the math. How important do you think you rank on his list of priorities?" Jon stated directly to Cyril.

"Jon you have really given me a great deal to think

about and I do appreciate your candor. I will talk with you later today. Do you have any plans for tonight, if not maybe we can hang out. I think I might need a friendly face to chat with," Cyril said.

"I am as free as a bird. So let's do happy hour and see what develops. Okay, don't be down in the mouth about this, you'll be just fine," he said.

"I'll talk with you later today to decide where we will do happy hour. Thanks Jon, and I will talk at you later, bye," Cyril said before put the phone on the cradle.

Jon put the receiver on the cradle. His mind drifted to Bella and how all this was affecting her. If she even knew that her husband was contemplating leaving her. He wanted to call her under the guise of a courtesy of the help group. Jon decided that he would wait for her to contact the office to make an appointment.

Claire walked into Jon office and noticed that he was preoccupied with himself. She almost left him to his thoughts. She knew that she had a long day and needed to complete whatever he needed, before she could concentrate on her tasks. Tapping on Jon's desk to get his attention, Claire stood there with her pad in hand ready for his instructions.

"How long have you been standing there? I was thinking about one of our clients and her, pardon my language, fucked-up situation. I need to speak with you about our Ivy Lane Project. I need to know the amount of time you can devote to the project and I need to consult with you concerning specifics of parents in various neighborhoods in the city."

"So, you want some insight into families in the 'hood?" Claire asked.

"That's not what I meant Claire," Jon lied.

"Jon, it is okay. I know where I live and the perception of most people. That is not the case on my street, but I understand your question.What specifics about parents in the 'hood?" Claire asked candidly.

"I need to devise a strategy for implementing the Ivy Lane Project. Do I interact with the children first? Should I plan a parent's meeting? Do you think they will be receptive to me? Dealing with the parents first seems to put me in an authoritarian role which is not the approach I would choose. Which plan do you think would suffice?"

"Neither," Claire stated frankly.

"Neither. What would make you make a statement like that?"

"They don't know you. They've just seen your picture in the paper with various projects. But they think of you as one of them."

Jon didn't know what 'one of them made reference, to.' They thought of him as an Uncle Tom or were they making reference to his sexual orientation? He hesitated before he asked Claire, "What do you mean, 'one of them'?" He sat there waiting on her response.

She stalled before telling Jon, "they just think of you as white man in a black man's body," Claire said.

"Claire! You have got to be joking. How could they think that with all the black, African-American or whatever we are called today, programs and projects I've worked with. All the boards that I've been on to help the cause," Jon exclaimed.

"See, that's just it, you are on the board, you are the chairman of a committee, but how many times have you been in the 'hood without an agenda?" Claire calmly asked.

"I get the point. People shouldn't be so judgmental, but I do understand," Jon said through clenched teeth.

"I have to devise a plan, so people will want the project even with my help. I'll be damned if I sit around and continue to watch kids get involved with drugs, not if I can help it."

"Well what is your plan?"

"I have to devise a plan, but you will play an integral role in the development of the Ivy Lane Project. I think I will have you approach the neighborhood and get some reactions about this type of project. Then we can develop a program that will fit the needs of the neighborhood. I can come in as one of your consultants on the project. This will be an opportunity for both of us. I can work without an agenda in the neighborhood and you can become a concerned parent that wants change in the neighborhood."

"That plan will work. So when do we get started?"

"Well the research can begin immediately. We want to get the project off the ground next month. If you can attend some neighborhood meeting to get a gauge on what's going on, then I can get the ball rolling from my vantage point. I will contact the community members and get them on task so we will be ready for next month," Jon exclaimed.

"Will I have to meet with the committee? If so, when is your next meeting?"

"Not to worry, I will get you an itinerary for the next few weeks. I hope you had a lot of quality time with the kids, because you want have time. A few of nights a week for the next few weeks you will have meetings."

"That sounds good to me. My kids are old enough to handle me not being home in the evenings, Mr. Knight."

"That right I forgot, your children are grown," Jon teased.

"I'm glad they are not around to hear that. They really think that they are grown, then I have to bring them back to reality. Praise God, I have two wonderful children. I am blessed." Claire sighed.

"You really are, your kids are terrific. Claire you have done a fantastic job rearing those children alone. I know it was hard at times, but you stuck in there and gave it your best. You have two great kids to be proud of."

"Okay, I've got work to do so I will step to my desk, do you need anything else?"

"No, but thank you very much."

Jon sat at his desk and waited for this first appointment to arrive. He'd put the Ivy Lane Project materials away and prepared himself for his client. He read over her case notes from the previous session to familiarize himself with her situation.

As he sat there reading it occurred to Jon that he had a small bag in his pocket. Should he before his session. Why not, he thought. He maneuvered his way down the hall to the rest rooms. Checking to make sure he was in the rest room alone, Jon looked for feet under all the stalls. He was alone. He went into a stall, took the small bag from his pocket and proceeded to inhale a bump from the tip of his car key. He bumped up each nostril and sniffed a little water. He was ready for his first session of the day.

In the reception area of Jon's office Ms. Jones paced back and forth, waiting for Jon to return. She was early, of course, but still impatient. Ms. Jones was always early and pressed for time. She needed to get in and out as quickly as possible. She always had some errands to run. Ms. Jones had a problem with patience; she had not mastered the art of hurry up and wait. That was her lesson for the day. Jon made her wait until it was time for her appointment.

"It's nice of you to join us today," Ms. Jones said.

"Now, now Ms. Jones, it is now time for your appointment. I'm sorry. Have you been waiting long? I hope I didn't incon-venience you too much," he lied.

"Okay, let's get started," she said before she entered his office.

"Go in and take a seat. I need to speak with Claire for a moment," Jon lied again.

"Jon you are incorrigible, but I love you for it. Now what do you need? Are you coming down with a cold? I noticed that you have been sniffling all morning. Do you have tissues in your office?" said Claire.

"Yes, mother, I do have tissue in my office. I don't know what's wrong, I must be allergic to something at the office," once again Jon lied.

Jon took a tissue from her desk and wiped his nose. He looked at the mucous, immediately dropped the tissue in the waste basket, his blood on the tissue. His mind raced did Claire notice the blood on the tissue? He looked to her for some reaction there was none. She did not indicated either way. Jon went into the office for his session with Ms. Jones.

Her session ended with no great revelations or major breakthroughs. His concentration was on the bloody tissue. This was the second time in two weeks that he wiped his nose and there was blood on the tissue. He needed to make an appointment with his doctor to have him check it out. He thought, not. He would go to a walk in clinic. He thought not, again. He decided that he would let it go for a week to see what develops. If the bleeding persisted he would make an appointment. He wiped his nose only mucous. He was relieved.

The rest of Jon's day was filled with more of the same, no revelations and no major breakthroughs. By the end of the day Jon was ready for a cocktail and a diversion. He called Cyril to check on plans for the evening.

"Cyril, where are we drinking tonight?" asked Jon.

"Since you're close to downtown, why don't I meet you at your place in about a half hour. I need to get out of these working duds and put on some jeans and a shirt. So I'll see ya then," Cyril said.

"Okay, bro, peace," Jon said.

Jon gathered his things and told Claire, "don't be here all night. Those files can wait until tomorrow. So git!" Jon said.

"I have one other file to close out and I'm out the door," Claire said.

"Good, have a good night and I will see you . . . in the a.m.," Jon said.

Jon walked to his car and put his thing in the back and drove out of the parking lot onto the main street on his way home. He arrived home, having fought the good traffic fight and prepared for his evening. He changed clothes and sat at his desk to open mail and pay bills. He noticed a letter, not a bill, with no return address. He looked at the letter and wondered who was it from and why wasn't there a return address. He opened the envelope, it was a hand written letter addressed to him. He saw that the letter was from Ian. His heart stopped. He was filled with emotion and sincere thankfulness. He read Ian's letter.

August 8, 1988

Dear Jon,

This is the hardest letter I've ever had to write. My body still aches for the passion and pure love we shared so many nights ago. I am sorry that I have not called you since our night of sheer joy. Timing is a bitch. I have met my soul mate in you. The sad fact of the matter is that what we shared can never be realized, again. I know you don't understand, but by the close of this letter everything you need to know, will be revealed. I can't say that I love you. In time, if we were given the opportunity to vie for our love I feel that we would both know genuine ecstasy.

Please don't think ill of me for writing a letter instead of calling or seeing you face to face. I accept that I'm a coward. If ever I am alone with you, well, you know what will happen. I can't tempt fate. So, the written word is the best I can offer. I hope that you will always remember our bond and never think that I don't hold a beloved place in my heart for you. I hope that there is a place within you that keeps the embers of our desire burning.

As I told you before I am involved in a relationship with a wonderful man. Yes, that was Enrique at the cafe. However, he has been diagnosed with AIDS and I will not, cannot, abandon him now. I do love him, but he does not, has never made me feel the sensation that just our embrace induced. He is the only man that I have ever made love with until you. He is battling pneumonia and a host of other AIDS related illnesses. It is difficult to watch a healthy robust man dwindle to a mere whisper of who he once was. That is why I cannot leave him and I will not continue in an adulterous relationship.   I told him about you and our night of passion. I did not want to hurt him so I told him that I needed sex, something that we don't share anymore. We share intimacy, which sometimes is more passionate than sex. I don't know his prognosis, however, I will stay with him until, forever.

You are a true sweet spirit and I'm in awe that I've met you. I will not write, call or see you ever again. If by chance I see you PLEASE respect my wishes and make no effort to see me! I want to remember what we shared and please don't ever make me regret making love with you and sharing my essence with you.

Love,

Ian

P.S. I feel that you are my soul mate.   I'm sorry that we could not make our spirits soar.

 The words pierced his heart and soul. The letter was a piece of pure poetry and Jon savored every word until he read the last paragraph. That paragraph devastated Jon and he could only cry and ask why had he been forsaken, to find his one true love and not be able to relish in that love. He felt like a child given a lollipop and allowed to taste its sweetness and having it stripped from his hands never tasting the sweetness again. Jon now experienced true emotional drainage. He was so dis traught that his only thought was to crawl in bed and sleep and cry. He could not control his crying. Each tear that fell drained more and more of his essence. He lay there, a mere shell of himself.   Bloody tissue and a broken heart. Jon could not understand Ian's betrayal. Jon vowed he would keep his love for Ian always. He was emotionally ravagedby the letter and he did not know how to deal with it. He was used to getting what he wanted. This was a new concept for Jon, one that he disliked.

In bed he started thinking about his life and realized that this was befitting revelation for him, he needed to know the heart-break and pain of a relationship gone wrong. The most frightening part was that he had only spent a day with this man, Ian, but he was captivated by him in every manner. Jon knew that Ian was his soul mate. Theirs was a relationship that would never be realized. Jon was broken and alone. He needed the comfort of a friend, and no one was there. He put Anita Baker's *Giving you the best that I got* CD and lay lifelessly, alone in his bed.

Jon was in bed for what seemed an eternity. There was a knock at the door. He got out of bed made his way to the door. It was Cyril. He took one look at Jon and asked, "what happened?"

Jon's eyes were swollen from crying and sleep. His clothes were wrinkled, he looked a mess.

"I had a bit of bad news and I having a difficult time with it. I'm gonna be all right," he confessed.

"What bad news? Are your parents okay? What is it, Jon?" Cyril asked concerned.

"Here, read this letter and you'll understand," Jon said as he passed the letter to Cyril.

"If this is this a dear John letter from Juan, what is your problem?" Cyril asked.

"No! It's from Ian," Jon said.

"Dear Jon, this is the hardest letter I've ever had to write," he read aloud. Cyril thought that the letter might be too painful for Jon to hear to he began to read to himself.

"No! Read it out loud. I want to hear you read the good part," Jon said.

He read the rest of the letter to Jon. With every word Cyril could see the pain the letter caused him. Cyril held his arms out to hold his friend. He had never seen Jon in this state before, and he was concerned. They sat on the couch, Jon cried some more. Cyril consoled him. He didn't know why he was in so much pain because of Ian, but he was.

Jon wiped his tears and recoiled himself from Cyril. He went to the kitchen to retrieve the small plate. He would not normally do cocaine in front of Cyril, he didn't approve. Jon needed to have his mind free from the reality of his jaded life. He made two lines of coke and sniffed them one by one he asked Cyril, "would you like a cocktail?" He indicated that he did, Jon made their cocktails and they talked for several hours about much of nothing.

At eleven thirty in the evening Jon asked Cyril, "do you want to go out or what?"

"Not really I think I just need to stay in and relax. I still haven't given Bruce and answer, that's something I need to think about," Cyril said.

"I think I' gonna stay in, too. Puffy eyes and a swollen face are not cute. I would get no attention looking like this. So I'm gonna stay in read for about an hour and then hit the hay," Jon said.

"Jon it wouldn't matter how you looked, the boys will still be all over you as per usual," Cyril stated.

"Yeah, you might be right, but how much longer will they find me appealing? I am getting older you know and I can't keep up with the children like I used, to," Jon said.

"Yeah right. You are not getting older and you will have the boys flocking around you for many years to come. I just wish that I could have the right one flock around me for a change. I always seem to seek out the closeted or the married men. All I want is a good man with his head on straight and feet rooted deeply in the earth, who is not afraid of his sexuality. Is that too much to ask for, Jon?"

"No. That is not too much to ask for, but you are not asking

105

the right questions. You need to understand the reason why you continue in a situation with a married man and not end it when you find out he is married. That is the real question. When you answer that, all things will become very clear as to why you attract that type of man. It may have to do with your own sexual views of homosexuals. But it is a question that you need to ponder and find some real solutions for, before you can meet Mr. Right instead of settling for Mr. Right Now," Jon counseled. Jon shared,"I know I have issues with relationships and that is something I have come to terms with. My relationship phobia stems from my family environment, but I can't allow my family's dysfunction to corrupt me from having a meaningful union. I haven't met the right person who is available for me. Cyril, I am so fucked up about Ian. I know you probably think that he is just another conquest, but it was different. We connected. We had a chemistry I have never experienced before. I could have fallen in love with Ian very easily. Enough of that sappy bullshit. Like I said before you need to ask yourself that one question and answer it honestly, then you can begin the healing," stated Jon.

"Jon, I know you know your shit and I do listen, but it's hard for me," Cyril confessed.

"What is the hard part? You meet a man, he is married, you leave him alone."

"That's easy for you to say, look at you. Handsome, intelligent and you have a great job that you love. You got it goin' on. Oh, I forgot and you got body," Cyril exclaimed.

He stood and said, "Jon, look at me. I'm overweight, average looking and the hate I feel for my job is transposed into my personality, I'm unhappy with my life as it is that. Is something you can not understand."

"Believe me, Cyril I do understand. Why do you think I am so obsessed with sex? That is my source of power. I feel that when I have sex it makes me feel handsome and powerful. I think I have average looks, so I can fully understand your point."

"Yeah, you can really understand my point. Look in the mirror, you are a handsome man and I don't care what you think of your looks, others have a different view." Cyril told Jon.

"It doesn't matter what other people think. Self image is the most important image. I think I have average looks and that is all I see when I look in the mirror."

"Jon, I do understand your point, but its hard to think you understand when you look like you do."

"You need to focus on the positive. I think you are an attractive man. There are a lot of guys that think you are fine just the way you are."

"Okay, okay you're right there are some guys that think I am fine just as I am," Cyril agreed.

"You'll be all right. Trust me. I know these things," said Jon.

"All right, Mr. Therapist."

"I am not trying to hear that."

"We have done enough introspection, outrospection and any other spection. Let's move on. Do you want to go out?"

"I think I'm gonna keep it in tonight."

"Oh, see all you need to do is make a phone call or two and your needs will be satisfied. I have to go in search of."

"No, I'm gonna curl up with a good book and call it a night."

"Well I don't believe it you staying in with a book. This is one for the history books," Cyril teased.

"Yes. I have some reading to catch up on. I do read. I'm also working on my Ivy Lane Project. So I have a few things to keep me busy."

"You better be Mr. Professional."

"Quit it!"

"I'm just funning with you."

"I know. So where are you goin' in search of?"

"I don't know. I might go home and call it a night. I do have to work tomorrow. I don't know I'll have to see where the wind blows me."

Cyril left and Jon was alone with his thoughts. He decided to do a little work on the Ivy Lane Project. He pull got out the file and read over his proposal. He needed to determine a strategy to allow Claire to be in the forefront with the people in the neighborhood. He would urge her to get involved with some of the local civic organizations or volunteer at the community center. She would need to be the contact person for the locals. He thought, *Claire will need some time off and she'll need to leave work early. So we need to get our files in order before the Ivy Lane Project gets underway. Luckily, we still have a few weeks.*

He put the Ivy Lane Project file back in his briefcase. Jon took a book from the shelf and prepared to read. He needed to make himself a drink and use the small plate. He put the book back on the shelf and put on Diana Ross's *To Love Again* album. He sat and let her soothing whispers bathe him as he reclined on the sofa. He let his mind roam freely. This was the best time of the day and normally he was out in somebody's smokey bar or club. Tonight would be different, he was not going out. He was staying in and relaxing, alone for a change.

This was the first night in weeks that he was all by himself and he enjoyed the tranquility. He had forgotten how to enjoy spending time with himself. He had become so consumed with conquest after conquest that he didn't even talk with his parents much anymore. He knew he needed to make some changes in his life and this was a good start.

He turned Diana over and made himself another cocktail. He returned to his isle, planted himself and continued to bathe. Her lilting voice gently engulfed the room. He allowed his mind to focus. He thought of Ian. How had he allowed their brief liaison to permeate his emotions so intensely? Ian was the first person in very long time Jon allowed inside his heart.

He thought about what was there about Ian that enamored him
so. He thought of the day and evening they spent together.
Their conversation about art, philosophy and their different cul-
tures. He needed to see Ian one more time. That was not to
be.

He had resigned himself to the fact that he and Ian would
never be. The letter confirmed Jon's worst nightmare about his
life. His one true love was gone and he had nothing. He vowed
he would be a different spirit. He would not let his diversions
dictate his life anymore. This was a new mantra that he intended to make true.

Thursday, August 11, 1988

The sun rays streaked across the room and shattered Jon's slumber. He rolled around in the bed. Today was the first morning in a very long time that he awakened by himself. He spent the night alone, no sex. He remembered his new mantra and was dedicated not to break his vow.

Jon knew this would be a difficult task because many people defined him based on his conquests, not his character. So did he in many regards. It was the harsh reality that Jon was known for his sexual exploits more than the content of his character. Dr. Martin Luther King, Jr. would not be proud to have fought the civil rights battle, only for us to become sexual predators. Jon did not allow many people to see the real Jon, who enjoyed art galleries, wine tasting parties and book festivals. He kept the real Jon hidden from most people, except his inner circle. He relished that most people thought of him only as a libidinous maverick, because more sex equated more power; at least that was his philosophy.

Deep within Jon's spirit he wanted people to understand him with all his complexities. However, he never gave outsiders an opportunity to know the man. People not knowing the real man would always be a source of dissension in his soul, one that would never be resolved. He was a man with a mission, not to be driven by his libido.

Jon got out of bed and made his way to the bathroom to take a leak. He looked at the face in the mirror. For the first time in what seemed like decades, he looked at himself and did not want to cry about his fucked up life. He was on the road to something better. He did not know where exactly, but he had started on a quest to live differently. Sex was the start. He had put his love life or sexual aerobics on hiatus. "Today is the first day of the rest of your life and what do you want to do with it?" he thought. "Well, I know that I will not allow my soul to be inhabited by any unpleasant thoughts. I will not think about Ian. I have to be strong and open my self to true emotion. I have been emotionally arrested for to many years. It is time for me to take the advice I've been spewing all these years," he said to the face in the mirror.

Revelations made Jon stop and thank God that he was able to know the error of his ways before too long. He looked closer at his face and was glad he could continue with life without Ian. He had only spent one day with Ian, but the time he shared with Ian was the real Jon allowing his real being to open and let someone in. Letting Ian in was a mistake, but Jon liked the way he felt for Ian and wanted to feel again. He looked in the mirror and said,"Whatever gods there may be, send me a man that will make me want to feel the joy that I felt with Ian. I know that sex is and can be fantastic, but I want passion and emotional bondage. Send me someone to, dare I speak it, love."

His mind was whirling with his new found sense of direction, at least in the way of love. He showered and dressed before he went to the kitchen for his morning line of coke and a cup of coffee. He looked through some of his bills from the previous day that needed to be mailed. He retrieved those envelopes and was out the door. He put his things on the back seat and was on his way to the office.

There was an article in the newspaper concerning a local big-wig politician, which happened to be one of The Help Group's A-list clients who used aliases because of their celebrity. The article reported that he was in therapy for manic depression and that he was on medication for his condition. The article alleged that if he were in deed a manic depressive and on medication, that maybe he was not suitable for his job. Jon went to his office relieved that the man in question was not his client.

"Jon, Mr. Hamilton needs to see you in the conference room. He's meeting with all the senior therapists," Claire said over the intercom.

"Thanks. I don't know how long this meeting will take, so see if you can contact Mr. Simms before he leaves home and tell him we need to reschedule his appointment," Jon said.

"I will call him. Is there anything else you need?" Claire asked.

"Yeah, not to have to be in this meeting," Jon teased uneasy.

Jon went to the conference room and took a seat. He and the five other senior therapists waited for Mr. Hamilton to arrive. No one spoke. They all sat with grim faces waiting for Mephistopheles' ascension to the conference room from the abyss. No one could anticipate his reaction. So they all prepared for the worst. The conference room doors flung open. Mr. Hamilton entered, slamming the doors behind him. All eyes watched his every move.

He stood at the head of the table and yelled at the top of his lungs, "How the hell did this information fall into the hands of a God damned reporter! He slammed down a file and exclaimed,"What the fuck are you doing? I thought you boys had your shit together? Smith talk to me! How did this bastard get this information?"

"Mr. Hamilton, sir, I'm not sure. I have never divulged any information to anyone about any client that I have worked with. This is the first time something like this has ever happened to me. Mr. Hamilton, I don't know what happened," Smith said.

"Smith you are on probation until this matter is resolved. That means you are not authorized to consult with any clients. Your case load will be divided between the other senior therapists. Is that understood? Check with personnel to see how much personal and vacation time you have; take it. You need to be out of your office within the hour. I will be by your office to make sure you are gone. Do you understand? Out within the hour?" he said.

Smith's demeanor seemed relaxed for the desperate situation that he was facing. There was more to his story that he was not sharing or he was genuinely unaware of how the information was leaked. Time would reveal. He continued to deny any knowledge of how his client's information got out of the office.

"Well, do any of you have any answers?" Mr. Hamilton exclaimed. The room was silent. All the therapists looked solemn and unsure of their futures with the help group. They all knew Mr. Hamilton had a temper, but no one had actually experienced any of his wrath since he had been with The Help Group.

"This meeting is over and your case load additions will be ready by the end of the day! If there are no other questions. This meeting is over, get back to your offices and back to work!" Mr. Hamilton said through clenched teeth.

"Mr. Hamilton, may I speak with you alone?" Jon asked.

"Sure, okay, see the rest of you later."

"With this in-house scandal are we going public or will we take a wait and see position?"

"Since we were not mentioned in the article we will just ride out the storm. Hopefully, this will end soon without any repercussions for the help group. I am at a loss for words. The board of directors were on my ass early this morning at home. So by the time I arrived at the office I was livid. This is the publicity that The Help Group does not need. Anyway, no, we will ride it out, Knight. Don't you want to know how this scandal will affect your pet project?"

"Yes sir. That was my next question."

"This incident will have no bearing on your project. In fact, if the newspaper exposes The Help Group in a follow–up article your project will be the best type of damage control. Rest assured your project is safe."

"Thanks."

Mr. Hamilton left Jon in the conference room and went back to his office. He sat there for a few minutes. Jon went back to his office and thought,"I need a bump after that meeting. It was extremely taxing." He checked his pocket and went to the bathroom. Checking the stalls to make sure he was alone. In a stall he bumped, to the sink for water and back to his office.

In his office Jon reviewed files and prepared for his next appointment, Mrs. Meadows. She was an elderly woman that had lost touch with reality or so she makes her children think. Mrs. Meadows is just a lonely woman in need of some attention. Mrs. Meadows and Jon had great sessions. She would tell him all about when she was a rebel rouser during the sixties. Although she never met Dr. King personally, she was in his presence on numerous occasions. Jon had encouraged her to join a senior's group or volunteer at her grandchildren's daycare center. She puts him off because she enjoys his company. She regard him as her other son. He reviewed her file and put in his in box. He had invited her children to attend a session; none had attended.

Jon wiped the moisture away from his nose mucous and blood stained the tissue. His mucous membranes were obviously broken or bruised which caused his nose to bleed. Nevertheless bloody tissues would not deter him from sniffing coke, not yet. He enjoyed the high and was not ready to live without it. He put the bloody tissue in the waste basket hiding it under some other discarded papers. He prepared for his session with Mrs. Meadows.

Claire buzzed Jon and said, "Mrs. Meadows is here. Shall I send her in?"

"No, I'll be right out to meet her," Jon said.

"Fine, I'll ask her to have a seat."

"Good."

He whirled his chair around and thought, damn I need to call my parents. I have allowed our relationships to diminish, for no reason. I will call them today. Jon went to his lobby and escorted Mrs. Meadows into his office. She sat on the couch he sat in a chair facing her.

"So how are we today, Mrs. Meadows?"

"I'm fine, baby. How are you?" she asked with a southern drawl.

"I'm doing well. Better now that you are here." he responded. He got his note pad off the desk and rejoined Mrs. Meadows and said, "Now, have you given any thought to my suggestions? I think you should get involved with more activities. This will give you less time to think about Mr. Meadows. Your children would welcome and encourage you to spend more time with your church group. You know that I'm right, don't you?"

"Chile, I ain't got time for more meetings. I'm busy as ever." she confessed. "No, I ain't gon' join no senior's group, but I listened to you and I took your advice. So, twice a week I'm gon' start down at the nursing home, volunteering. I'll answer the

phones and sort and deliver mail to the folks in the home. You
were right it does make me feel good. My children don't want
me to volunteer at the day care center with my grand babies. So
I went to another one with AIDS and crack baibes, I go there
once a week. I'm just gonna hold the babies, but I feel like I got
a purpose," she said as she rocked on the sofa. She was beam-
ing with pride once again, she was of use to others. Mrs.
Meadows would not feel useless and unwanted again. Her session was about over for today. She knew that her children
would not be pleased with her volunteering so much, she
decided not to tell her plans and that would be that.

Jon informed Mrs. Meadows,"I will not schedule another
appointment with you, okay? If you think you need to talk call
me and we will set an appointment. Mrs. Meadows have great
day and call to let me in on your activities."

Mrs. Meadows said,"I'll call you just to say hello and tell how
I'm doing with all my activities." She left his office and he felt
better because of the progress they had made during the past
year. When he called his first meeting, she sat and did not say
anything. It took about three sessions to get her started and
when she started the flood gates opened, which was a wonderful thing. He would miss their weekly sessions. Months ago
he should have moved them to twice a month, but Mrs.
Meadows would not hear of it, and anyway she enjoyed their
sessions.

He buzzed Claire to tell her,"Don't schedule Mrs. Meadows.
I am putting her in the pending case load." He leaned back in
his chair and thought, I should call Cyril to check if we can do
lunch, it has been such a long time, since we'd shared lunch. He
picked up the phone and dialed Cyril.

"Cyril Mansfield, may I help you?"

"I don't know, can you get away for lunch old buddy old pal?
Its been a great while since we've done lunch. Can you get
away?"

116

"Sure, where do you want to meet?"

"You make the call, I'm flexible."

"How about Johnson's diner? I feel like some down home soul food today."

"Twelve thirty?"

"Make it one and were on."

"One it is. If you beat me there order me some lemonade? And if I beat you, iced tea. See you at one."

"One. Peace my brother," Cyril said and put the phone on the cradle.

Jon leaned back in his chair and decided to call his mother. Her phone rang four times before she answered the call.

"Hello," she said with Georgia twist in her voice.

"Hey, ma its your favorite son."

"You're my only son and yes you are my favorite. To what do I owe the honor of this call?"

"I had been thinking about you for a few days and thought I should call to see how you were doing. I met with a client this morning whose children have all but abandoned her. I didn't want to think I was that way. So, I decided to call to say hello and let you know that I still love ya."

"I love you too, baby. You all right? Sounds like you got something on your mind? You sure you all right?"

"Yeah ma. I am fine and I don't really have anything to talk about, I just wanted to let my mother know that I loved her and I proud to be her son."

"Boy, what's wrong? You are being to, I don't know, ya being to something."

"Like I said my client this morning got me to thinking about our family and how we need to spend more time together. I don't come home for visits that often and when I do I'm in and out over the course of a weekend. That's not fair to you guys. I should spend more time with you and daddy."

"Baby, you got a life and you need to live it. We done lived

117

our lives. Now, its your turn. Baby, we know you love us. Coming home more often will not make you love us more. Long as I know that my baby boy is fine, then I'm fine. Baby, come home when you can, don't beat yourself up about it, now. See, I remember when your grandmother made such a fuss about us coming to her house all the time. There was nothing wrong with that, but she never wanted to come to my house and so I finally had to tell her, 'Mother, would you please come to my house for a visit?' She never knew how much that bothered me, her not visiting us. So, baby, tell people what you want them to know. Don't assume that they know, nothing. Make sure they know by telling them, all right baby," she said.

"Listen at mama, gon' withcha bad self."

"All right boy. Don't have me come up there"

"Have you seen the old man lately?"

"What have I told you about that?"

"I'm kidding, making a funny ha ha...ha." Jon said.

"No ain't seen and ain't looking for him. He out tending to his garden I guess. So, boy what's on your mind?"

"'I'm making some changes in my life."

"After your changes ... will you still be gay?"

"Ma!" he moaned.

"I can ask, can't I? You said change and..."

"I know Ma, no that's not the change I meant,"

"Well, a mother can hope that this will not afflict her son forever. You said change."

"I'm sorry you misunderstood. Ma, I'm gay and I will be gay until the day I die. That's just a fact. And I make no apologies for being gay. The powers that be made me gay, I accepted it and lived."

"All right baby what kind of changes?"

"Just how I live. I'm gonna find someone and settle down. Stop ripping and running up and down the road to party. I'm simplifying my life."

"Good, I am so tired you calling from New York, Atlanta, or some other place and you didn't even tell me you were goin' anywhere. You need to settling down. Thank God. Boy, I worry about you all the time. Where is he? Is he all right? Why don't he call us more?"

"Ma, you know I love you and daddy. Don't worry about me, I'll be just fine. I am opening my eyes to the future and looking at a bright path."

"I pray all is well with you my son. Love you,"

"Love you, too. Ma, tell Dad I call him tonight and I love him. I need to get out of the office. Talk with you soon."

"Bye baby."

Jon leaned back in his chair to collected his thoughts. He reached for the phone and dialed his father's number in the office/utility shed. His father did not answer the call. He left a message. "Dad, just called to say hello and I love you. I will call you tonight like I told mama." He checked the time. It about one and he needed to meet Cyril at Johnson's. He prepared to leave the office. He told Claire, "I'll be back in an hour or so. I should be here before my three o' clock appointment. If not, have them wait. If I'm not back by ten after reschedule the appointment. Thanks, Claire. How was your lunch?"

"I will do as you asked and my lunch was fine, thank you."

He took the elevator to the first floor and went to the parking garage. He got in his car and sped off to Johnson's Diner. He hit every light and was there in record time, about eight minutes. He pulled into the unpaved parking lot. Cyril's car was there. He went in the restaurant. He spotted Cyril and Bruce at a table. He was taken aback. Jon had not expected Bruce for lunch. He waved and made his way over to the table.

"Hey, guys how are you . . . two? " Jon asked reluctantly.

"I'm fine. Guess who was here for lunch? So I invited him to join us. You don't mind do you?" Cyril probed.

"Fine, we will have a wonderful lunch, just the three of us.

So how the hell are you Bruce?" Jon asked sarcastically.

Jon was not pleased Bruce joined them for lunch, but what could he do? The trio would have lunch and that would be that. Jon thought about Bella and felt a sense of betrayal on his part. There was nothing for him to do but endure lunch and get back to the office.

"I'm doing pretty good. No need to complain, don't nobody care. How have you been?" Bruce said.

"Doing well and you are right, no need to complain, nobody listens," Jon said. He gave Cyril his patented I-don't-believe-this-shit look. Cyril received the message and looked through Jon so as not to feel the penetration of his stare.

"You are right, we haven't done lunch in a long time. I'm glad we made a date for lunch. What a coincidence to run smack dab into. . . ," Cyril was cut off by Jon.

"Bruce. Yeah, just us three a nice cozy lunch," Jon said dryly.

The waiter came over to take their orders. He was an elderly gentleman, maybe sixty-five or seventy. He wore navy blue Dickies work pants, a short sleeve plaid shirt and a pair of brogans. His salt and pepper hair reminded Jon of his grandfather, who passed when he was in college. Jon still remembers the night his father called with the news of his grandfather's death. Jon cried the rest of the night, mainly for the shitty manner he had treated his grandfather when he was alive. The older gentleman made sure there was silverware and water on the table. He brought our drinks to the table.

"Thank you sir," Jon said.

"Welcome," the older gentleman said.

Bruce said, "Jon."

"Yes."

"Did Cyril tell you? I'm leaving my wife?"

He looked to Cyril for confirmation and answers. "He might have mentioned something to that effect. So, you are leaving your two little children alone with their mother?"

"It's not like that," Bruce said.

"Well are you taking the kids with you?" Jon asked.

"Jon, stop it," Cyril said.

"No, he's right I brought up the subject. No,I don't intend to take the children with me. I'm leaving my relationship with my wife. I plan to be very involved with my children."

"What made you want to leave your wife in the first place?" Jon probed.

"I am gay. I have come to terms with that realization. No longer will I live a lie. So, the best thing for me to do is leave."

"Have you and your wife discussed this matter? Have you considered a marriage counselor a preacher or both? There must have been a time when you loved your wife, wasn't there?" Jon questioned.

"Yes, I loved my wife very much, but she could never give me what I needed. I needed to be held and loved by a man. I knew I was gay, but my family . . . and society taught me that I should get married and have a family. So, I did." Bruce confessed.

"Look at the lives you have ruined," Jon stated as he stared through Bruce. "I pray that there are no long term repercussions for your children. Your leaving needs to be handled with the utmost care for their well being. This can cause emotional scars your children may not reveal until they're adults. So, please consult with a licensed social worker to help prepare the children before your departure," Jon counseled Bruce.

"My wife's been seeing a therapist, she said we would have to see another therapist, not hers. Maybe she can schedule time for the two of us, with a marriage counselor. Do you think that is a good idea?" Bruce asked.

"Very good idea. Can I ask you a question, Bruce?" Jon asked.

"Why stop now," Bruce said.

"Why?" Jon asked.

"Why, Why what?" Bruce asked.

"Don't play me. Why did you marry her when you knew liked dick?" Jon asked.

"I thought that I would be able to stay away from men. I did very well the first three years then I met this one and all hell broke loose. My wife caught me in bed with Cyril and put me out of the house. I got back in the house and I have been faithful until about a year ago. Again, I ran into Cyril and . . . ," Bruce admitted.

"The rest is history. Now, can we please talk about something else. I want to, Bruce wants to and this is what you do for a living," Cyril chimed in.

"I'm sorry Bruce. The whole gay married man syndrome has and will always fascinate me. I have never understood it or will I ever. But, we live in America and people are free to make their own decisions," Jon stated.

"Jon, move on. Give it a rest." Cyril said.

"You are right. So, Cyril what's up for tonight? You wanna hit it?" Jon asked.

"I might be busy, tonight. I'll call you later to let you know. Right now I'm not sure."

The waiter brought there food to the table. He made sure all the glasses were topped off and asked, "does anyone need anything?" The trio indicated they did not need his services at that moment. The food on the table looked delectable and tasted the same. They all ordered the smothered chicken, special of the day.

"Cancel that Cyril I'm staying in tonight to read," Jon said.

"Really now? What kinda a boy stays home alone, a boring one?" Cyril asked.

"Yes, really. Boring as it may seem, I need to catch up on some reading for the Ivy Lane Project. There are some other grants that I need to review and see if my project is eligible. I have put it off long enough. So, tonight's the night for work."

"Well, what are you doing tonight?" Cyril asked Bruce looking at Jon in disdain.

"Nothing, I'll be home with the family. My son is working on a school project and I promised that I would help. So, I'll be home tonight," Bruce indicated.

The trio remained silent for a few minutes, enjoying their lunch. Each had other thoughts on their minds. Jon's mind was on his own the situation at work and how the Ivy Lane Project would effect the rest of the therapists. Cyril was contemplating his answer to Bruce, whether he should allow him to move in. Bruce was pondering his life without Bella and the kids; partying all the time, all the men he wanted and no more curfews. Bruce envisioned a charmed life.

"Truth or dare, Bruce?" Jon teased.

"Truth, I have nothing to hide," Bruce responded.

"Jon, are you going to the dance on Friday after the football game? Jon we are not in high school. Truth or dare, come on?" Cyril exclaimed.

"Bruce do you have a problem with my question?" he asked.

"Not at all," Bruce replied.

"Well Cyril you may join us or we will play without you," Jon retorted.

"No thank you. I'll sit this round out. I've seen this play before and I hate climactic endings," Cyril sneered.

"Come now, Cyril, join us. You have always been a engaging ingenue," Jon cajoled.

"Exit stage left. Bruce I will talk with you, whenever. Jon, I will give you a call this evening and maybe we can do something. Oh, I forgot you have reading, but we will talk later. Which check is mine, well it doesn't matter we all had the same thing. Peace out my brothers," said Cyril as he left the table and went to the counter to pay his bill. He turned to his table mates, waved a last goodbye and was out the door.

"Truth," Bruce tested.

"I was just kidding about the game."

"No you weren't. You were about to ask me something about my wife. Anything to make Cyril look at me in a bad light."

"Got me! You are ab-so-lute-ly correct. I can't help it. If I see my friend in the deep end of the pool, I throw him a life preserver. I get crazy. He deserves more than you have to give." Jon explained.

"You don't know what we share . . . ," Bruce said before he was cut off by Jon.

"Look, its not that I don't like you. You seem like a nice guy and all, but you have a wife and two children. Why are you fucking with my friend's emotions? Do you know the best thing you can do for Cyril? Leave him the fuck alone," Jon interrupted. He stood and picked up the remaining checks on the table leaned over and whispered to Bruce, "I'll take care of your lunch. Can you do one thing for me? Leave Cyril alone! Have a nice day my best to the family." He walked to the counter and paid for their lunch and was out. Bruce sat and drank his iced tea.

He walked in the office reviewed his messages. There was a message from Bella. He was intrigued and immediately called her.

"Hello," she said.

"Hello, Mrs. Toussaint this is . . . ," he said before he was interrupted.

"Jon, I must make an appointment to speak with you. I need your advice and I mean now!"

"When would you like to come in? Better yet, why don't you speak with Claire and she will set you up with my next opening and I will speak with you then. Hold on," he said as he buzzed Claire. "What does my afternoon look like?"

"You were booked solid, but Mrs. Cooper cancelled. So, your last block of the day is open," she informed him.

"Great, I have Mrs. Toussaint on the phone put her in that

time slot. Hopefully, that time will be good for her."

"Will do," Claire said.

Jon waited for Mrs. Toussaint, Bella, to arrive for her session. He wondered what she needed to speak him about and why she sounded so urgent on the phone. Did she want to talk about her relationship with Bruce? Was she ready to move on without him? His mind went over the various scenarios. He decided to put her situation to rest. She would be there soon enough with all or at least some of the answers. He leaned back, in his chair remembering that he had not spoken with his father and needed to give him a ring. He thought, I'll call him tonight when I get home. So we can catch up. Jon's mind wandered to his talk with his father about his sexuality.

The evening was like many in his hometown, the sun was setting across the big lake and its brilliance shimmered over the water making beautiful diamonds that danced on the water. Jon sat on the rocks and watched the magnificence of God's artistry. The crystal blue lake merged into the grey sky at dusk to create a fantastic portrait of day's end. Empty picnic tables reminded Jon of happier times, the Fourth of July fireworks and times just swimming in the lake with his father. Neighborhood gossip had made its way to Jon's father's ears. He and his father had not talked, but he knew it was only a matter of time. Jon was so consumed with his own being that he did not hear the truck pull up behind him. Looking out over the lake he was startled by a deep voice.

"Mind, if I join you?" his father said.

"Huh," he said, looking distracted from his own world.

"Do you mind if I join you?"

Jon realized that his father was with him at the lake and it was time for the talk. He wanted to tell his father to leave so that they could talk later, but he knew that the time was now and his father would not take no for an answer.

"You can sit right here," Jon said as he moved to let his father sit. He didn't know whether to bring up the subject or to let his father broach the topic in his own manner. He tried to figure out the best way, but his father had an agenda.

"Son, you know that I love you . . . and will always love you. No matter what you do, what you are? If you were a criminal, I would still love you. I will always be your father and love you no matter what. So, just remember, I love you and will always be your father."

"I know," Jon whispered. He sat looking out over the lake through tear stained eyes. His face was wet from crying. He didn't say anything to his father for a long time. The father put his arm around his son. He leaned into his father and was glad that he had his support, if not blessings. They never brought up the rumors that his father had been told, although both knew that the stories had an element of truth. Neither spoke the word 'gay' or 'homosexual', but it was understood that there would be no grandchildren. Father and son sat on the rocks for hours. They listened to the waves crash against the rocks. They did not need words. That was the first time Jon realized how much he loved his father, for no other reason than being his dad. He would never know how deeply wounded his father was that his only son was gay. He was mortified, but would never allow his son to know how much sorrow his homosexuality had caused him and his mother. Jon and his father arrived home late for dinner that evening.

His afternoon appointments were uneventful, but his used his idle time contemplating the plight of Bella and what she wanted, needed his advice for. Had she found out about Bruce and Cyril? Had Bruce confessed that yes he was having an affair and with the same man you caught me with three years ago. Soon enough all would be revealed to him and he would question no more.

"Jon, Mrs. Toussaint is here shall I send her in?" Claire asked.

"That will be fine," he said. He was beside himself with anticipation of her news. He didn't have to wait any longer. Mrs. Toussaint had arrived.

"Hello, Mrs. Toussaint. How are we doing today? May I offer you something to drink?"

"Only if you can offer me a Kamikaze. Otherwise, no thank you."

"Sorry, we only have coffee and soft drinks," Jon apologized.

"Then like I said before, no thank you!"

"Please, have seat and we can get started," Jon said reaching for his note pad. He sat facing Bella.

"Now, what is it that you need to discuss with me?"

"Jon, I don't know what to do. Bruce, my husband, and I had a long talk just last night about our relationship and our family. We both only want the best for our children. He is moving out at the end of the month. The children don't know, yet," Bella confessed.

"I'm sorry to hear that, Bella. I wish the two of you could have worked something out. Have you thought about one of our marriage counselors. I can still make a referral. Is there no possible reconciliation for the two of you?"

"Jon, Bruce is gay! My husband is gay! I don't have the right equipment. I can no longer go with the flow. When he didn't go out and flaunt his shit in my face, I was cool. Like I told you about a year ago it started. I forgave him for cheating on me with a man in my bed! I was such a fool, but my children needed a father, or so I thought. So, I laid down the law and we moved on. We tried to make it work. I should've never believed that he would change or keep his sexuality under wraps. What a big ass fool I was."

127

"You gave him the benefit of the doubt after you put him out. I do remember that conversation. You were not a fool. Your reaction was normal. So, what do you plan to tell the children? How do you plan to tell them?"

"That's one of the reasons I'm here, to get some help. How do I tell my babies that we're getting a divorce?"

"Is there absolutely no way for you to work things out?"

"Jon!. Hello, are you listening to me? Bruce, my husband, is gay! He wants a man. I feel like such a failure. I can't even keep a man! What good am I?" Bella exclaimed.

"Focus, Bella. The man in question is gay and there would have been no way for you to keep him. He was wrong and inse-cure about his sexuality. You did everything right. You were upfront and truthful, he was dishonest and underhanded. You can hold your head up that you were a good wife to him. Even after he cheated with a man in your bed!" Jon screeched. "You were too good for him!"

"That all sounds good, but bottom line my husband would prefer to be with a man than to be with me. Can you make that different? Can you make my husband want me? I didn't think so,"she said. Bella's eyes filled with tears. She took a tissue and wiped her eyes.

"Jon, I don't know what to do. I'm falling apart here. It was not supposed to be this hard. I still love that son-of-a-bitch. Why? I don't know, but I do? Tell me. . . something . . . any-thing!" Bella cried. She looked to Jon for answers that she already knew. She needed to move on with her life, but was afraid that she was not capable of being the strong, independent woman she thought she was. That was one of the reasons she allowed Bruce back in the house. She was afraid, but with the current twist of events she would have to stand on her own two feet and make it happen for herself and her children. Her tear–streaked face looked at Jon. He watched her silent plea for help.

"Bella you will make it through this. First, do you have a lawyer? If not, I know some excellent divorce attorneys that can help. Second, when you last spoke with your husband, you decided that he will stay until the end of the month, correct? During that time you need to sit down and start to iron out some of the financial responsibilities. Who pays the bills?"

"I do."

"Perfect, then you know where the money is?"

"I won't have to worry about money, Bruce has always been fair and I work. Do we have to talk about this stuff?"

"Unfortunately, we do. I know Bruce has been a wonderful husband about taking care of the family. That was before. Before, he was not living in the home and out in an apartment, paying rent. Buying his own food. Paying the bills. Picking up his own dry cleaning. When all is said and done, he will not want to give you adequate money to care for the kids. I would suggest that you get with your attorney as soon as possible. Give him as much information about your husband's financial situation and let him proceed from there. I have seen it too many times; good husbands in the house go bad living outside the house. Talk to your lawyer as soon as possible."

"I will. Bruce and I will sit down and discuss our plans for the children, how they will be cared for and by whom."

"Okay, we've gotten financial and divorce issues out of the way. Was there some other reason you wanted to see me?"

"No, I just needed to talk with someone who would not be judgmental. Someone detached. You seemed like the perfect candidate, so here I am."

Jon was very distressed by the Bruce and Bella and Cyril triangle. Cyril promised that he and Bruce were over and would only be friends. He prayed that Cyril could keep that promise. There were other lives hanging in the balance of his decision. Jon did not feel that it was a good idea for Bruce to be roommates with Cyril. That would create a tense situation for Cyril, one that Jon did not want to deal with, in any manner. He sat across from Bella and thought about the times he'd shared with Bruce and his lover, his dear friend Cyril. Jon felt a bit unethical, but that would not deter him from continuing to see Bella as long as she wanted to talk.

"I wish things were different. There is a part of me that wishes he was not gay and would want to stay married. Unfortunately, that is not the case. Is there anything I can do for you, Bella?" Jon asked sincerely.

"You have done enough. I thank you for being my therapist, but also a friend, something I needed more than a therapist. I didn't really ever think that you and my husband were. . . you know? I needed an excuse to talk with a professional, as fate would have it there was your
card."

"Thank God you found my card. So, I hope all goes well with you and hubby. I pray that all will work out for the best, for all concerned," Jon replied. He gave a little hug as she left his office. She was on her way to a better life without Bruce, thank God for that. Now, if he could only convince Cyril that he'd be better off without Bruce, then he would be content.

Another day ended and he was on his way home. He remembered to take his Ivy Lane Project materials with him. He told Claire. "This doesn't seem right. I always leave before you. That will soon change," as he patted the Ivy Lane Project folder.

She stated, "I can't wait."

"Neither can I. Have a good evening and don't stay too late."

He continued down the hall to the front of the building and the parking garage. He put his things in the back seat and was on his way home. He was not going to happy hour or seeking any other diversions. He drove through Orlando and made it home safely.

Jon put his work things on the desk and proceeded to the bed-

bedroom. Once there he took off his clothes and slipped into a pair of silk pajamas and went to his desk. Jon stopped in the kitchen to make a cocktail then on to his desk. He picked up the phone and dialed home.

"Hello," his father answered.

"Hey old man. How are you doing?" Jon teased.

"Fine son, I'm better now. Your mother told me she spoke with you today. I felt a little slighted that you didn't speak with me, but she told that you were calling me tonight. So, I sat in here to wait on your call."

"Dad, like I told ma today. I was just calling to tell you that I loved you. Nothing else really. There was a client today that made me think about family. I know I don't visit often and when I do I in and out. When I'm there I'm in Miami during the evening. So we never get a chance for a real visit. I plan to do better. I know mama done told you all of this, but I think that you need to hear it from me, too. Daddy, I was thinking about the day you came to the lake and sat with me."

"What made you think about that, it has been so long ago."

"We never talked about the rumors and we never mentioned gay or anything, but I knew that you knew. I am just so grateful that you did not react to what was in your head. I am blessed that you responded with your heart. Father, I know it is not easy having a gay son. I know the pain and anguish you and mama had to deal with. I am sorry that you had to engage in all of my drama. I am proud that you didn't kick me out the house and denounce me as your son. I will always be grateful for your kindness," Jon confessed.

"Son, as I told you that day on the rock looking out at the lake, I love you no matter what. You are my flesh and blood. I would have never put you out of our house. No, I don't understand why my only son had to be gay. Son, we loved from the day you entered this world and we will love you, even from beyond the grave I will love you."

"Thank you, daddy. I know how painful my being gay is for you, but I'm proud you are my father. Daddy, I love you," Jon said as he got choked up at his own emotions.

"Okay, enough of this mushy stuff. What about these changes your mother was telling me about?"

"Oh, I am not going to party as much and I will settle my happy self down some."

"Thank God, your mother worries about you and so do I. We never know where you are. You calling us from all over the world. We love you and we want you to be happy, but try to stay in one place?"

"That is a part of the change. I will let you all know when I leaving and where I am going so you won't worry so much."

"Good, now how's our boy Cy?"

"Cyril is fine dad. He tries to keep me in line, but that is like the blind leading the blind," Jon teased.

"We're glad that you have him there. You both need somebody to look after ya. Tell him that we said hello. You remember Mr Hudson?"

"You know he was on trustee board for 'bout the last thirty years, anyway he passed the other day. They had his funeral yesterday. All his children came and the cried something awful. None of them ever came to visit. That's what they cried 'bout. How pitiful they were as children. They just had abandoned him. If it wasn't for your mother and me, well I don't know. Anyway. I'm gonna let you go. I'll talk with you soon, son. Remember, we love you."

"I love you, too. I will call more often, okay. Love you, bye." Jon said and hung up the phone.

He reflected about their conversation. He knew that he was blessed with the world's best parents and he was glad that his parents, were not like Cyril's who turned their back on him when he came out at twenty-one, loved him.

He opened the Ivy Lane File. He read through the file and

highlighted areas that needed additional work and other areas that needed to be italicized and bulleted for the city proposal. Additional funding or in-kind donations were needed to develop the Ivy Lane Project city–wide. Jon was pleased with the outlook of the project. There were a few more pieces needed to get the project off the ground.

Jon was in contact with the mayor's council, county art's council, Urban League and the NAACP. With these agencies sponsoring the project there would be no way for the program to fail. He would make the necessary phone calls tomorrow to put the final pieces in place. Jon was gratified that The Help Group would allow him to take time, resources and Claire for his pet project. The Ivy Lane Project was destined to be a huge success and he was proud to be a part of the process. He completed his Ivy Lane review and put work away.

Diana Ross' voice was needed to make his evening complete. He went to the stereo and put on her, *To Love Again*, album. The volume was at a mellow level. Then he went to the kitchen and made another Tanqueray on the rocks with lime and pulled the small plate from the cupboard. He sniffed the cocaine and put the plate away. Jon went back to the living room and plopped on the couch. He sat and let her sultry lyrics pour over his body. Jon pressed the button on the answering machine and listened to the messages.

Juan left several messages. One, he wanted to know when was he coming to New York and had he made reservations yet? Two, Why hadn't he called him, just to say what's up? Third, were his feelings still the same, friends? Jon responded to the night air, "Yes I'm still coming to New York, no I have not made reservations and yeah, you are still a friend."

Mel left a message, "Yo', this is Mel. Remember me? I can still feel you inside me. When can we do it again, soon I pray?"

"Sorry Mellie Mel, that was a one shot deal. No, we can't do it again, but keep praying we all need His help," Jon whispered

133

to the answering machine.

"Hello Jon, this is Ernest. I just called to say hi. I . . . um . . . well if you ever have any free time you can always give me a call. I'm usually at home, if not please leave a message and I will return your . . . ," Ernest said before he was interrupted by the beep. He did not call to complete the message.

"You are a nice guy and all, but you were just a fuck. Nothing more, nothing less, just a fuck, sorry. One shot only. No repeat performances," Jon said out loud.

"Jon, yo' this Eric, sorry I just need to release a little. Man, that bitch don' lost her fucking mind. She don' went and left me. Jon, she packed her shit and left. No explanation, no nothing. I ain't gon' be lookin' 'round O-Town fo' her ass. She don' los' out. I am a good bro . . .," he said before the beep interrupted him. He called back, "I am a good brotha and she know it. I don't know what she looking for, but I am the best she ever had and she gonna regret leaving me. I ain't gonna look for her, either. He paused. She . . . probably at her mama's house, later, Jon."

Jon had no response for Eric. He knew that Eric would do the right thing if he really loved Kelli and if not he would lose out on a good woman. Since Eric mentioned Kelli's where-abouts that suggested that she was important to him, although he didn't like to admit it to many people. Jon could see through his charade. If he didn't care he would not waste time talking about her and how she makes him mad all the time. If she caused him that much distress he would have broken up with her by now. Eric and Kelli would be fine.

Jon picked up the phone. He needed to speak with Cyril. They had not had a chance to talk about lunch yet. He dialed his number and waited for him to pick up.

"Hello," Bruce said.

Jon was so dumbfounded that he hung up the phone and sat at his desk stunned. He did not expect Bruce to answer Cyril's phone. Jon needed to collect his thought before he could call Cyril again. After all the talking he and Cyril had done concerning Bruce and the notion of a possible relationship, he never thought that Cyril would let Bruce move in. He was so outdone that he went to the kitchen and made another cocktail and had two lines of cocaine. He collapsed on the sofa and let the alcohol and cocaine infuse his brain. The infusion was complete he picked up the phone and called Cyril again.

"Hello," Cyril said.

"Hey, what's up?" Jon asked.

"It is not what you think. I did not invite Bruce to move in, I was in the bathroom and I asked him to answer the phone. That's it end of story."

"You are a grown man. You know what you're doing. I just called to tell you that dad asked about you, when I spoke with him earlier. That's it, nothing else. Like I said you are a grown man and you know what you are doing," Jon replied with a questioning tone in his voice.

"Jon, Bruce is not moving in with me. He and I had that discussion and I thought it best he live somewhere else. Not with me. You and I had this conversation the other night. We both made pledges. I thought that my word was enough for you?"

"Not when it comes to men. Your word is not worth the air you breathe to speak it. I should have given you the benefit of the doubt, but I couldn't. I know how much you love married men and Bruce is one," he said.

"Touche, damn that smarts. Why, oh why do you always have to . . . be right?"

"Because it my job, Blanche. Its my job." Jon teased.

"Okay, so what's up? You want to terrorize Orlando tonight? Oh, I forgot you are staying in and working, right?" Cyril queried.

"You are absolutely, one hundred percent correct, I finished my Ivy Lane Project review and talked with my daddy. I listened to some messages left by some people you might know. Ah, Juan, Ernest and Mel."

"Juan wants to know when you're coming to the big apple. Ernest just wants to be with you again. I don't think I know Mel?" Cyril questioned.

"Remember the other night we were out and that boy that came up, tapped me on the shoulder and said he was . . .," Jon said before Cyril interrupted him.

"Going to sleep with you tonight. Oh, I remember Mr. I-want-the-notorious-Knight. You must have put it on that little blonde kid good?"

"Can I do it any other way? I don't think so. Yeah, he left a message he was praying for some more of the notorious Knight. Damn, I'm good. I'm just good!" Jon exclaimed.

"Well, since you have done your home work are coming out to play? Come for a little while?"

"Is Mr. Mr. coming out with you? Anyway I thought he was supposed to help his son with a school project? What's up with that? Not even out of the house yet and already neglecting the children," Jon said not wanting to neglect himself.

"You've got it all wrong, they completed his assignment earlier. Bruce decided that he would come over after they had completed the school project. Back on you, are going to wreak havoc on Orlando with me tonight? Come on please." Cyril pleaded.

"No, I'm staying in, because if I go out I will be tempted to bring home a snack, of the human persuasion, a young tasty morsel. But, I will not make any progress by keeping myself away from temptation. Cyril, I will go out, but I will not stay out late," Jon conceded.

"Great, we'll have a ball, boy. This will be like that one time you were on your no sex kick. We would party like animals and we had a hoot!"

"I do remember and I gonna put on my boogie shoes and be

ready for you. Cyril, it is 10:30, what time do you want to meet at Southern? I am ready to party, sugar."

"Midnight is the bewitching hour, so let's make it then. I will see you at the bar."

"Peace, my Brother and tell Bruce go home, bye," Jon said and put the receiver on the cradle. Jon pondered what Cyril and Bruce would do before he met him at Southern. He quickly put that thought out of his mind and moved on to other more pleasant thoughts. He went to his bedroom and looked for something to wear to the club. He decided that, since he was not out looking for sex, to put on a pair of baggy black pants and a black shirt.

Before he dressed for the club he took a long relaxing shower. He adjusted the water temperature, just below scalding. The water ran for a few minutes, he stepped into the pounding stream. He relished each droplet as it pelted his body. He stood braving the waters. Jon loved hot showers almost as much as he loved sex. He lathered his body and purged himself from the impurities of the day.

Jon finished his shower and lotioned his body. He sat in the bathroom on the counter and massaged himself. He rubbed and squeezed every part of his body that he could comfortably touch. He sprayed some Perry Ellis cologne and walked into the mist. A trick one of his girlfriends had taught him it seemed to work, he always smelled good. He dressed and was in the kitchen making a cocktail and doing some coke before he left for the club.

The black Mustang zipped along the interstate as Jon listened to Prince's Head, blaring from the speakers. He was so engrossed with sniffing a bump, that he did not realize that it had been raining and there were puddles on the interstate that could cause cars to hydroplane. He continued down the interstate in the direction of Southern Nights. He was traveling faster than the speed limit. There were other misguided souls on the interstate who, like Jon, did not obey the speed limit.

Jon put the corner of the matchbook cover to his nose and sniffed. He closed his eyes to let the cocaine by pass his bruised or ruptured mucous membranes en route to infiltrate his brain. His eyes opened to a display of fire works as a car spun on the interstate. Luckily, the maniac driver was too far ahead of Jon to have any impact on him. He saw the metal scrape against the concrete median causing the mini-meteor shower. He was barreling down the interstate, he had to swerve to miss the fiery car. He looked in his rearview mirror and continued on his way. Jon would have stopped, but he had alcohol on his breath and cocaine in his system. Had he stopped to help he might have been on his way to the detox unit and then jail. He was sorry he could not help.

He made his way to Southern Nights sliding into a parking space across the street from Southern Nights. He met Cyril outside. They hugged and went inside to the pulsating sounds of Madonna's Burning Up. They went straight to the dance floor and started their night of dancing and drinking. On the dance floor Jon tried to tell Cyril of his harrowing experience trying to make it to the club. Cyril could not hear, so Jon decided to tell him later. Southern was unusually crowded for a Thursday. Cyril and Jon danced up a sweat and then went to the patio bar to drink and rest.

"Baby, let me tell you what happened on my way here tonight. Some poor child damn near killed herself. I mean the car was spinning around and sparks were everywhere. Honey, I had pass right on by that girl 'cause you know a little hooch on the breath and powder in the system. I would have been calling you from downtown," he said. He got the bartenders attention and ordered, "Tanqueray on the rocks with lime and a Captain Morgan's and coke, please. So, I hope that child is okay. I couldn't stop. I couldn't take the chance."

"I understand what you're saying. I don't think I would have stopped either. I can't put myself in a detrimental situation."

"Well, what happened with Mr. Bruce. He can't stay with me. I don't want to have anything else to do with him, but you see him twice in one day. What's up with that?"

"Like I said, he called and asked if he could come over. I said sure, why not? Yes, I still want him, I will not deny that fact, but he is married. I am trying to get off the married man merry-go-round. Remember we talked about that the other night. Me off married men. You off men period, for a spell?"

"Oh, I remember it was when I saw Bruce today at lunch it took me for a loop. I was not expecting to see or hear from him so soon after our no more Bruce conversation," Jon confessed. "Then tonight when I called your place, he answered the phone I was absolutely speechless, so I hung up the phone. I didn't know what else to do!"

"Nothing at all happened with Bruce. That is the way I wanted it and he had to understand and respect my position, which he did. He did not try to pressure me into doing anything. We talked and I left for the club and he went home, I guess. It really doesn't matter where he went. He and I can only be friends as long as he is married," Cyril insisted.

"Just remember one thing he cheated on his wife with you. She had his two children. If he cheated on her he will cheat on you, believe that."

"I know he cheated, but that was because it was a woman and not a man, right?"

"Cyril, now I know you know better. Cheating is cheating is cheating it doesn't matter the gender, baby. The fact is he cheated, period."

"I know. Well, he will only be a friend and nothing more." Cyril said hopefully.

"Why does he need to be a friend? Listen to the scenario, he will call one night to hang out with a friend. You are horny, he comes over to hang out and you end up in bed. Then where do you go from there?" Jon probed as he looked directly into Cyril's eyes.

"Okay. Okay, I understand, but Jon, I need to make this decision for me. I know what is best for me and that is what I will do, okay. I not stupid. And stop looking at me like that."

"No one said you were stupid, just vulnerable when it comes to unavailable men. You always want men that cannot make a real commitment to a gay relationship. That's at the root of all of your relationship fiascos. I don't want to have a session with you, but right is right. That is where you are, deal with it," Jon retorted.

"Jon, you didn't have to go there, but since you did and once again you are right! Why? Why do you always have to be right? Don't say because its your job either!" Cyril yelled.

"No, I'm a voyeur of relationships. Watching relationships go bad from the outside, you can see where they go wrong and who is at fault. My opinion is that all involved parties are at fault to a degree."

"So, you've watched me, tell me?"

"No, I have told you on numerous occasions. I just told you a few minutes ago. Weren't you listening? See, that's your problem right there you don't listen to me when you need to. You need to stop going after men that are not open to gay relationships. That include married men and men that only come to you house for sex, you know, trade. Men like Bruce should not be in your life. Look for a gay man, a man that is gay and does not have a lot of baggage, wives or girlfriends or children."

"But, I want a real man. You know what I mean?"

"That is a part of your hang up right there. You feel that if a man is decidedly gay, then he is not a real man. That comes from your upbringing, about sissy and fag conversations you were privy to as a child. You need to get that mentality out of your head and realize that gay men are real men. They are as

140

real as any other man."

"I don't think that way? Do I?"

"I just read it as it is written in the book of Cyril. That is what I see, so that is what I say."

"Enough, psychology 101. We are here to party. I will make an appointment with another therapist, I wouldn't be objective with you. I'd keep saying that you trying to run thangs. So, let's party, baby!"

The animated allies went back to the dance floor to kick up their heels. The music was pumping and they were feeling their moment. They cleared the dance floor with their wild antics, they were on a mission to enjoy themselves and from all accounts that is exactly what they did. They danced for thirty minutes before they were winded and returned to the patio bar. No psychology 101 this time around; they were at the bar to consume cocktails.

Jon fought diversions all night long. There were so many attractive men out so he plunged himself into dancing and drinking. He was determined to stick to his vow. He and Cyril danced and drank until Jon was ready to go home alone. Cyril was impressed that Jon had not pursued anyone tonight. Jon gave no attention to those that flirted with him. Jon prepared to leave, but Cyril decided to stay. They hugged and said their good byes. Jon left.

On the ride home Jon took his trusty matchbook cover and cocaine pouch from his pocket and did a bump. That lasted him until he got home. It was 1:30 a.m. and Jon was a bit wired from that last bump. He decided to do another bump and call Juan to chit chat.

"Hello," a groggy heavy Puerto Rican accented Juan said.

"Hi, Juan this Jon. How are you? I just wanted to give you a call to let you know that I was thinking about you. I have not made any reservations yet. I plan to come up there in September. Probably around the end of the month. I have this project that I'm working on and it will be up and running by that time and I can take a few days for a visit. Will you be able to take a few days off when I come up? I need to know just in case, so I can hang out with my girlfriend, Dawn who lives in Brooklyn. But if you can take time off then I will just stay with you and not worry Dawn I need you to let me know whether or not you are taking time off from work so I can let her know what my plans are? I still think about your visit to Orlando and I want to feel your body next to mine as soon as possible. But, I will call you to let you know the exact dates that I will be in the Big Apple. I'm sorry for calling so late, but I just walked in the house and wanted to give you a call. I will talk with you later, bye," Jon said and hung up the phone. He had spoken so quickly that Juan did not get a chance to say a word except, hello.

The cocaine had accelerated Jon's body reaction to a point that he was rushing around his apartment cleaning tables, lamps, chairs and talking to the sofa and other living room furnishings. He raced about the room talking incessantly. Jon felt some snot drip from his nose. He wiped away the mucous and it was more blood than mucous. He blew his nose and more blood and mucous was released. The more he blew his nose the more blood was on the tissue. He wiped his nose again and the blood saturated the tissue. In his irrational state he threw this tissue away and allowed the more blood than mucous combination to flow; he used the back of his hand to wipe away the bloody mucous. Then he wrenched his hands looking at the pristine apartment, but his drug induced mind's eye saw a mess.

"My God, look at this mess. I've got to clean this rubble before anyone comes to see me. Jon, now you know we don't keep our house in disarray. Faggots keep immaculate homes. You are letting the sissy boys down by not being tidy," he said. He continued dusting the furnishings frantically after he used the dust cloth to wipe his bloody nose. "Look at this streaking.

Jon, how can we get the streaks off the table the more I wipe the more streaked the table gets? I don't know and why the hell you asking me, anyway?" he said. He continued to deface the living room with his blood.

The room was void, no voices or music penetrated the silence that engulfed the room. Jon's living room was in total upheaval. Picture frames were on the floor. The furnishings were smeared with blood and mucous. There was a pungent odor from Jon's hysterical cleaning frenzy and the smell of blood. Alcohol and cocaine had taken its toll on Jon and he lay lifelessly between the sofa and coke table. The small plate was on the table with cocaine lined up and a cocktail waiting for Jon to emerge from the floor. The cocaine and cocktail went unused.

Friday, August 12, 1988

The Help Group's office was buzzing with another article exposing yet another local politician being accused of being treated for a psychological disorder. This time the accused was not an A- list client of The Help Group. The article was an expose on two fronts, psychologically unfit politicians and breach of security with a local transcription company.

Mr. Hamilton had called Smith to inform him that he was allowed to come back to work and extended an apology, but reminded him that the situation and the board of directors warranted his reaction. By 9:30 a.m., the office was calm and back to normal. Jon was late for work again.

Claire called and canceled his two morning appointments and decided to give Jon a call to make sure he was coming to the office after lunch or at all today. This was a regular routine with Jon, so she called his apartment. The phone rang and rang, there was no answer. She left a message," Jon, this is Claire. I have cancelled your two morning appointments. Um, if I don't hear from you within the hour I will cancel the rest of today's appointments. This concerned Claire, Jon was usually at home or had called to let her know how to handle his scheduled appointments. She went into his office and pulled the files for the remaining clients for the day. Claire worked for the next hour, since she had not heard from Jon she called and rescheduled his appointments.

Jon's apartment was vacuous of sound. Silence orchestrated a symphony of hushed concertos for the furnishings in the apartment. No voices interrupted the quiet. Jon's body lay lifelessly still on the floor between the coke table and sofa. His face was plastered to the carpet from dried blood and mucous. His body had not moved since he collapsed the night before. The floor was his resting place.

Jon's phone rang and rang. He could not answer. Cyril left a message,"Man, why aren't you at the office? I know that you went home alone last night, so what's up? I'm glad I stayed I met this hot gorgeous man last night. He came home with me and well . . . you can guess the rest, but I want to tell you about my night," Cyril said before the tone interrupted him. He thought to call back and complete his message that the man he met was gay and out, but decided not to. He would speak with Jon later, so they could make plans for that night.

Late Friday afternoon the sun pierced through the blinds and showered the living room with warm summer rays. The sunlight hit Jon's face with a vengeance and his crusty eye opened and closed quickly from the brightness. He opened his eyes glued together with matter. His face was stuck to the carpet; he slowly pulled his face away, stinging. He felt the side of his face and could feel the dried blood. His body was stiff and sore from sleeping on the floor, between the sofa and coke table. The living room looked like some crazed killer had run amuck and left his calling card, smeared blood everywhere. Jon's hands were covered with dried blood and mucous.

Struggling to get up Jon leaned against the sofa. He looked around the room in horror, not knowing exactly what happened. The longer he leaned against the sofa, more tidbits began to trickle into his mind, and he saw himself trash his living room, the night before. He felt under his nose and scratched away the dried bloody mucous. Jon looked at the clock and realized that it was 4:30 p.m., but he didn't know what day it was. He did not know how long he had been out. This was the first time in a long time that Jon had blacked out, but he vowed that this would be the last time.

He called information and determined that today was Friday and that he only missed a day of his life. He checked his messages and knew that he needed to contact Claire and Cyril. Jon called The Help Group. "Claire, this is Jon. How are things there? Was I missed today? Please tell me you rescheduled my day? I know that you did, but I like to ask." Jon said, through a thick, alcohol–coated and lethargic voice. He sounded very tired and still asleep.

"I rescheduled your day when you were late for your morning appointments. Mr. Washington was very angry, but we rescheduled his appointment for next week. All and all it was a fairly quiet day."

"Is there anything that I should be aware of that happened today?"

"Have you seen today's paper?"

"No, I'm just coming to?"

"Well, another local political big wig was in the paper about needing mental help, but the article exposed the woman who leaked the information. She worked for our transcription agency. So the morning was a bit crazy, but after lunch everything calmed down and was back to normal."

"Good, did Smith come back to work?"

"No, but Mr Hamilton sent around a memo that he would be back on Monday."

"Good, I'm glad all this has blew over and all is back to normal. Claire, I need you to make referral for me."

"For which client?"

"Not for a client but for me," Jon said softly.

"For you?" Claire said, knowing that he has needed help for some time, now.

"Yes, I need a appointment with Joel."

"But, Joel is our subst . . .," she said before Jon interrupted her.

"Substance abuse counselor, I know . . . and I know that you've known for some time that I needed his help. Sorry for putting you in an awkward predicament. But please make the appointment and as per usual, keep it under your hat. I know I don't have to tell you these things, I just like to hear myself talk sometimes."

"I'll make the appointment. I will speak directly with Joel to set up something after hours. Okay, I will do that immediately."

"Thank you, Claire. I thank you for being a wonderful assistant. That Ivy Lane Project is coming along just fine and maybe I will have some very interesting news for you Monday. You have a wonderful weekend and I will see you early Monday morning."

"Jon, take care of yourself and I will pray for you and your situation. Have a good weekend and I will talk with you Monday morning, okay."

The offensive stench permeated Jon's nostrils. He looked at his living room in utter amazement that he had created such chaos. His clothes were ruined with bloody mucous. He examined the tables, sofa, lamps and other furnishings to determine if he could clean them properly. He looked a himself in a mirror with disgust. How had he allowed himself to descend to such depths of madness. Jon was dedicated not duplicate last night's behavior, ever again. He needed to clear his head and make a fresh start. He decided he would visit his parents for the weekend. Jon took the next few hours and cleaned his apartment from top to bottom. When he finished his Hazel routine he called Cyril.

"Hello, speak," Cyril said.

"Hi, bitch, how the hell are you?" Jon asked.

"Slut, fine. Now, where the hell have you been? I called you at the office and at home today you were nowhere to be found. I thought you were on sexual hiatus or have we changed our minds and gravitated back to a life of decadence? I'm listening."

"No, I have not gravitated back to a life of decadence. Although last night was pretty wild, to say the least, but tell me about mister mister from last night, thing!"

"No you didn't take me there. No you did not call me thing, as in Ms. Thing?" Cyril shrieked.

"If the pump fits. If the pump fits. . . wear it," Jon teased.

"All right. I won't let you have it right now, but it is on the way. Well, let me tell you about mister. I was pretty trashed, but then I saw this guy that was very attractive. So, I thought to myself. Self, what would Jon do in this situation? So, I marched right up to him and started a conversation. Now, you know it was awkward because I'm not as suave as you, but we get to talking and one thing led to another. He is decidedly gay. He is single and looking. He is not married. I repeat he is not married. We just had a fabulous night together. I even pulled a few of your tricks, candles, ice, and of course baby oil. Baby, when I brought the baby oil out mister went up. In more ways than one. Jon, we had a fabulous time and we are getting together tomorrow night. Jon, I hope that Matt is the one, at least he is not married. Thank you God!"

"This sounds like it could lead to something. How does it feel?"

"It feels pretty good. We just met, but there seems to be a chemistry, a connection," Cyril shared.

"Cyril, I hope that this is all that you want and need it to be. You deserve happiness and I hope that Matt can help bring that to your life."

"I do, too. Okay, mister where were you all day?"

"I was here," Jon confessed.

"Screening our calls are we, why?"

"Not screening exactly."

"Then, what exactly?"

"Remember the other night when I decided to leave. Well, I did some coke on the way home and the stuff was quite potent. It got me pretty wired. But, when I got home I did another line or three, I don't really remember," Jon said before he was interrupted by Cyril.

"Jon when are you going to quit that shit? It is not good for you or anyone else." Cyril said genuinely concerned.

"I know, I counsel people everyday with all types of addictions. You would think that I would know better. But anyway, like I said, I did some more coke when I got home. That is when everything gets a little fuzzy. I remember cleaning my place in a frenzy, like a madman. My nose was running from the coke so I kept wiping my nose. Only thing it wasn't just snot, it was blood, too. I mean I had blood everywhere on the sofa, tables, lamps, on the walls well you get the picture. The last thing I remember was talking to myself about cleaning the apartment before people came over. The next thing was waking this afternoon. I blacked out and missed the entire day. Thank God I was alone. I mean this scared me. I've blacked out before but this was the first time I've been destructive. I can't let this happen again."

"Jon, what can I do? Is there anything I can do to help?"

"Thank you. Cyril, all you can do is just what you are doing, be my friend. Listen if I need to vent. Be who you have been to me. Cyril, I love you and I am blessed that I have you in my life."

"I love you, too. I am just happy that we became friends. You are my brother and your parents, thank God, excepted me like their own. I am the one that is blessed. Your family took me into their hearts and care for me, unlike my family, who turned their backs when I told them I was gay. You and your parents are my family. I am truly blessed to have you in my life. Like I said, if there is anything I can do?"

"Cyril, thank you. There is nothing you can do. I have to do this myself."

"Okay, what are you doing tonight? Let's go to dinner and a movie?"

"That sounds like a plan. I need to get out of the house anyway. Let's check what's playing at the Ezian?"

"Sounds good. I will check the time and call you right back, okay."

"Ciao, baby."

Jon put the phone on the cradle. He waited for Cyril to call with the movie information. A diversion was needed and a movie seemed to be what was in order. He hoped that the Ezian was not showing a foreign film with subtitles. He did not want to read tonight. Looking around the apartment in amazement, Jon was pleased with the difference a few hours made regarding cleanliness. Jon looked at his shirt and remembered that he had not taken a shower and he smelled. He called Cyril to tell him that he would call after his shower.

Jon went to the bedroom pulled out some khakis and a polo shirt for the movie. He went in the bathroom and adjusted the water temperature for a nice hot shower. Looking at the man in the mirror, he was not afraid, he did not feel the need to cry about his fucked up life. Jon knew his life was getting better for the mere fact that he was showering without a companion. Making a vow to halt his sensual propensities. Looking at his face, he really saw himself. And for the first time in a very long time he saw Jon. A man with a new expectation of life. Knowing that he deserved better than he had given himself. He showered and called Cyril.

"Cyril, I have completed my shower and I will meet you at the Ezian, tell me what time does the movie start?"

"The movie starts at 10:30. It's an avant garde flick about existentialism or something deep shit like that. Anyway it will get you out of the house and open your mind to something new."

"That sounds good to me. I will meet you there about 10:15, okay."

"It's a date."

Jon placed the receiver on the cradle, went to the cupboard and retrieved the small plate. He emptied the contents of the pouch onto the plate. He took the razor blade and cut and sifted the powder. Jon formed two thick lines of coke and sniffed then up quickly. He took the small plate and place it in the sink and washed the remaining contents down the drain. He put water in his nose for the last time from snorting cocaine. He tolerated his brain to be pierced once again from the effects of cocaine. His mind was reveling in the wake of the coke, but Jon had decided that this was how he wanted his last cocaine experience.

Cyril waited outside for Jon to arrive at the Enzian. Jon parked his car in the parking lot and walked across the lot and greeted Cyril with a big hug. They decided to get some refreshments before the movie started. Cyril ordered a glass of zinfandel and Jon a cola and some buttery pop corn. They both did some people watching before the movie started. The room faded to black the screen lit the room. The movie began. The lights came on and the movie was over.

Jon went home, listened to some music and had a cola on the rocks with lime. He went to his bedroom and packed some clothes for the weekend with his folks. Of course, he had to take a suit for church Sunday, there was no way around church. Jon didn't really care that he would attend church, he thought that it might be a good thing. He finished packing and went to sleep. He rested well.

Saturday, August 13, 1988

Jon woke up early anticipating his trip home for the weekend with his parents. The sun was not up, yet. Jon made coffee and sat on his balcony to behold one of God's daily miracles. The sky was a charcoal grey and the morning air was crisp and cool. On the horizon was a faint glimmer of what seemed to be illumination. The trees, grass and flowers were moist with dew, which made them all appear to have on velvety sweaters to warm them from the sting of early morning. As a sliver of brilliance gleamed from beyond the horizon, Jon felt serene. Half of the sun had pushed its way up from the depths of darkness to make a new day. The rays of the sun raged over the city like a tidal wave drenching everything in its wake. The trees, grass and flowers were losing their velvet, the dew

153

drops evaporated and descended into the soil. Jon was at peace.

Jon pulled into the driveway and parked his car. His mother was sitting on the porch and his father was working in the yard. When she saw her son she beamed with pride that her son had come home for a visit without prodding, just because. His father saw his son pull into the drive way he put his rake down and looked at his wife and was glad. Jon jumped from his car and ran to the porch to hug his mother. They embraced. His father came from the yard and they also hugged.

"Son, why are you here? Is everything, all right?" he said.

"Baby, are you okay? The other day when we talked you sounded like you had something on your mind. Are you all right baby?" she probed.

"Mom, Dad I'm fine. I just needed to see to two most important people in the whole wide world to me. That's it. I needed to see my mommy and daddy."

"Now, if something is wrong, son, we are here for you." he said.

"Dad, everything is fine. I needed to get out of the city and spend a relaxing weekend. What better place than to come home and see my folks? You guys have any plans for today? I think we should take a drive over to West Palm Beach and along the coast or something."

"Maybell, we ain't got no plans today, do we?" he asked.

"No, we don't have any plans, Carl," she responded.

"Then its settled. We will take a drive along the coast and check things out like we did when I was a kid. The difference, I'm driving and we will stop for a burger when I'm ready!"

Father, mother and son laughed. Jon gathered his overnight bag and garment bag and took them to his room. His mother left his room the same way he left it ten years ago. He put his bag on the twin bed and hung his clothes from his garment bag. He sat on the bed and thought about all the nights he'd spent in this room thinking about his future and where he would end up.

In his bedroom everything seemed so much smaller than he remembered. The bed, definitely. The bureau drawers looked to be about half the size they once were. Even the ceiling seemed lower. Jon was home. He remembered the night he and his mother had the talk about his sexuality, days after he and his father spoke at the lake.

Maybell Knight came into her son's bedroom like a whirlwind as she always did. She was a lady, elegance and style. The look on her face was not one that Jon recognized. She looked pensive and hurt. He did not know what to think and then like a ton of bricks it hit him. His mother knew, no grandchildren. What was he to say or do? He sat and waited for her to open the obligatory can of worms. She danced around the subject for quite a long time for her; normally she waltzed in and asked the question. This question was too difficult and personal, so she bided her time.

Her soft voice with the Georgia twist asked in her matter-of-fact tone, "Baby, are you funny? I . . . heard these rumors and I don't want to believe them, so I'm asking you to ease my heart and tell mama those rumors are lies. So I can git on with my life."

He stood to respond, "Mother, I don't ever want to do anything that will in any way hurt you or cause you any pain or embarrassment, but I will not lie to you. I don't know exactly what rumor you heard, but I am a homosexual and that I can not change," Jon said as he looked up at his mother standing beside his bed.

She stood there and the tears streamed down her face. He was her child and he would have to suffer the taunts and misfortune of being one of them; a faggot. She was beside herself with rage and hatred for the person responsible for making her son different. She could not speak. She wiped the tears from her face and looked at her son.

"Mother, I'm sorry. I don't know why I'm gay, but I am and I can't change it. It is just who I am."

She slapped Jon hard across the face and screamed, "You are not! You are not! You are not one of them faggots. Not a child of mine, you are not a damn faggot!" She grabbed Jon and shook him violently as if to remove his homosexuality. She slapped him again and again. She pushed him away from her. He fell across the bed hitting his head on the headboard. She fell to the floor sobbing and chanting, "my baby is not a faggot, my baby is not a faggot, my baby is not a faggot."

He rushed into the room and picked his wife up and took her to their bedroom and laid her on the bed. He went back to Jon's room to check if his son was okay. He was fine, but cry-ing uncontrollably. He sat his son on the bed and put his arm around him.

"Son, your mother loves you very much. She just needs some time to get used to the idea that her child, her son, her baby is a homosexual. Your mother will come around. Are you okay, son? How's your head?" he asked. He rubbed his son's head and face and told him, "Everything will be all right just wait and see." He left to check on his wife to make sure she was doing okay.

Jon knew that things would never be all right with him and his mother; she would never accept that fact that he was gay. Although she would tolerate it, she would never accept it. Jon and his mother never spoke of the incident and they went on as if nothing had transpired between them. She continued to mend and darn his socks and was a wonderful mother to him. All was as it would be for the rest of Jon's life. She would never accept his homosexuality, but she would never disrespect him or his sexual orientation. She loved her son and did not want to lose him.

Jon put away the things from his overnight bag and went to the den. His father was back in the yard and his mother was in the kitchen on the phone with her girlfriend, Maxine He looked out the window at his father diligently making sure that his yard was well manicured. He took great pride in the fact that his yard was well maintained. His parents relationship didn't seem different from when he lived at home, he assumed they were just content with each other. He thought that they were too old to go out and find new mates, so they made a decision to stay together.

Actually, his parents had fallen in love again and were very happy with each other. He saw their love for one another on their trip to West Palm Beach. They were very attentive to each other, so much that it made Jon realize what he was missing not being involved in a real relationship.

He asked his parents, "What happened? You two seem so . . . happy, what happened?"

"What do you mean? What happened? I love this woman, she is my wife, remember."

"Yeah, this is my man. I love this old man and we are happy."

"I remember all those years when I was growing up and you two didn't seem so . . . happy."

"Well I'll tell you a few years ago, Bro. Watson died. He was a single man with no one in his life and I decided right then and there that as long as I have this beautiful woman in my life I would treat her the way she deserves to be treated, like a queen. I apologized to your mother for all those years we argued and treated each other like . . . well, shit. I told her as long as I was alive I would give her the respect that she was due. From then on we have been like two peas in a pod. I just adore your mother. I'm sorry for all the years we lost being nasty to each other, but I try to make it up to her every day."

"That's right baby. Your father and I have been like two kids on their honeymoon. Bro. Watson's death really made us examine our life together. We looked at all the years we lost for no reason. We both wanted the same things for all those years, we never sat down and talked about what the other wanted. We never talked. We yelled and screamed and had sex. Now, after all these years we make love and it is beautiful."

Jon interrupeted, "Okay, that's more than I need to know."

"No, your father makes me feel like a school girl. That's what I was telling you the other day. We have lived our lives, but each day our love gets better and better. Jon, baby, I hope you find someone to make you enjoy the dawning of each new day. If you find someone half as good as your father you will be doing just fine."

"You . . . want . . . me to find a man, mother?"

"Son, you have to live your life in the manner that will make you happy. If a man will make you happy then find one, settle down and be happy. That' all a parent ever wants for their child; happiness. I only hope that you don't waste too many years looking for love like we did," she said.

"Well, I did met this one person, man, wow, man, that I could fall in love with," Jon confessed.

"What seems to be the problem?" she asked.

"He is involved in a relationship. We've only spent one day together, but there was a connection, chemistry that was undeniable. Unfortunately, he wrote me a letter and told me that he never wanted to see me again. The letter crushed me, but I'm coping."

"Son, we're sorry you have not had a good time in the romance field, but look to the Lord for guidance. If someone is out there for you, it will happen. The two of you will be together," she said.

"Look, son things will work out just fine, pray for guidance like you mother said," he said.

"I've been praying a lot more lately than I have in a long time. There are some things happening in my life that I need God, a

Higher Power or whatever to help me, because I'm going through. I know that I will be fine, I just hit a rough patch," Jon shared.

"Son, it will be all right," he said.

"I know. I am so surprised and thrilled with the two of you, though. I remember all those fights when I was growing up. Ya'll were always arguing and fussing. I thought ya'll didn't love each other. One time I thought my relationships didn't work because of my examples, but I know they didn't work because of me."

"Son, we are so sorry we put you through all those years of agony, because of us being thick– headed. You needed us to show you a loving home. Sorry we couldn't show you that, then. Jon, we love you and we have done you a great disservice. There is nothing we can do about it now. Except to tell you that we are sorry for our behavior and only wish that we could make it up to you," she said.

"That's right son. We have talked about this and we were sup- posed to do something special for you to let you know how deeply sorry we are for making your life a living hell. We know it wasn't easy with us as parents. Here we are now the best for you and now you don't need us," he said.

"Please don't ever think that I don't need you. I love you and will always want and need you to be the best parents alive. For a long time, I was very angry at ya'll. I did not understand how you could love each other and me, but fight all the time. It was a very confusing time for me. I got to a point where I didn't care one way or another. Ya'll could love each other or kill each other it didn't matter to me. As I grew older I realized that what- ever the two of you were going through, it had nothing to do with your caring about me. When I got that understanding, it didn't matter how much you two carried on. I knew that I loved you no matter what."

"This is nice. I love the way we can talk about everything

and put it all in perspective. We are all coming to a greater knowing of each other and ourselves," Carl said.

"True, we are blessed. The Lord has opened our hearts to each other and just look at where we are, talking about everything under the sun," Maybell said.

The family continued to talk about Jon growing up, vacation nightmares and Jon's party attitude. He mentioned that he always heard them fighting even the time when they were trying to be quiet. They laughed and enjoyed their afternoon drive along the coast. On the drive home Jon's mother made a big deal of stopping by Sister Josephine's house; she had not seen Jon in years. They stopped for a visit. She still had the same furniture, from fifteen years ago. Nothing had changed in her life except she had a new television set.

After leaving Sister Josephine's house the family drove home. Jon went to his room to unwind from the drive. His parents went to bed. It was late, 10:30 p.m., they needed to get up early for church in the morning. He was not sleepy, so he decided to sit on the porch for a bit to relax. He stared into the night. The night sky was a luminous navy blue with silver speckles that shimmered like diamonds thrown across black velvet. Spectacular was one way to describe to night sky. He peered in awe of the beauty that was night. He smelled the night and was one with it. He went inside and went to sleep. His slumber was that of a newborn babe, gentle and restful.

Sunday, August 14, 1988

The morning came gently misting Jon awake to the smell of bacon, eggs, coffee, toast and cinnamon rolls. His eyes opened and his nostrils were filled with the wonderful aroma of breakfast. He was glad he was home and happy about his parents' new found romance. He made his way to the kitchen. His father was reading the newspaper in the living room and his mother was finishing breakfast.

"Breakfast is ready," Maybell said as she placed plates of food on the table.

"Everything smells wonderful. I can't wait to dig in," Jon said.

"You know your mother is a good cook, my mama taught her all she know about cooking," Carl teased.

161

"I ain't even gonna entertain you with that," Maybell said.

"I'm just funning with you sugar," Carl said as he kissed her on the cheek.

"Okay, you two in the kitchen let's get to the food," Jon said.

The family sat down at the dinner table for breakfast before they made their way to church. Jon's parents went to Sunday school. He decided not to attend. He would meet them at the morning service at 11:00 a.m. Jon toiled around the house that morning looking for something to do before church. He found his old high school yearbook and began to skim through, laughing at the fashions and hairstyles of the late 70's. He could not believe that his parents let him leave the house looking so ridiculous, but at the time his clothes were the rage. He looked at his trophies and ribbons from track team and the marching band. He enjoyed high school immensely. He looked at some of his school pictures and could only howl at himself. He put away his high school memories.

Jon put on his suit and was out the door, headed to church. He had a few minutes to spare, so he drove to the lake to become one with nature. Then he could join the congregation in a wretched rendition of *Amazing Grace*. He sat on the rocks as he had done many times before. He looked out over the lake and wished that there was someone for him out there. He wanted someone that was available, unattached. Jon wanted what his parents have now. He so enjoyed watching them together, seeing the genuine love they shared. It was an awesome sight that filled his heart with joy. Looking out over the lake he wished for a portion of what his parents had and half the time shared with someone he loved. He was beginning to get a little down, so he decided it was time to head for church.

The choir was singing, *An Uncloudy Day*, one of Jon's favorites hymns. Jon found a seat next to his mother, her choir was not in service today. His father sat with the Trustees and Stewards, financial and spiritual leaders of the church, respectively. The choir finished the hymn in a rousing throaty finish from Sister Mayes. Rev. Weaver rose to begin his sermon, the church quieted to hear the word of God. He began his sermon with a whisper and concluded with a crescendo. Rev. Weaver sat in the pulpit exhausted, drenched with sweat. They took up a collection and church was over.

The Knight family sat down for Sunday dinner. Mrs. Knight had cooked that morning all of her son's favorite dishes. The table was filled with southern delicacies. Mr. Knight said grace and the family commenced eating. They conversed about the sermon, church members and their holier-than-thou attitude. They enjoyed the rest of their Sunday dinner and rested the remainder of the afternoon, as is with most African-Americans after they have eaten.

Late afternoon, early evening Jon packed his car getting ready to head back to Orlando. Jon kissed his mother good-bye and told her that he would call her to let her know that he made it back to Orlando in one piece. Jon hugged his father and they said their good-byes. Speeding off in his car, Jon was off. He went to the lake for a last look before leaving his hometown. He looked out over the splendor of the water and sun fusion. His car parked under the trees, he pondered what the future held for him. He hoped someone would come into his life to make his life complete. He did not need anyone to make him complete, just his life. One last gander at the lake and he drove off; Orlando was his destination.

Jon had made it safely to Orlando and was feeling a bit hungry, he decided to stop by *the cafe* for a snack. He pulled into the parking lot and parked his car. He went inside and was relieved that "the cafe" was not crowded, as it was on some Sunday evenings, that last minute date before the work week began. The host directed Jon to a small table near the bar. A handsome man was tending bar, it was not Ian. Jon did not acknowledge the bar tender, he remembered the last bartender and the pain that liaison caused.

He sat at his table and ordered his dinner and a cola with lime; he was determined to quit his vices one way or another. Although, there was an overwhelming desire to order a Tanqueray on the rocks with lime, his better mind made him choose cola, instead. This would be a desire that he and his therapist would battle starting tomorrow, although he seemed to have it under some control. He ate his dinner alone. Jon looked around the room for a familiar face; there were none. Making mental notes concerning the Ivy Lane Project, Jon contemplated his work week. The project was only weeks away from beginning and there were still some loose ends that needed to be tied. He had received confirmation from all of the support organizations except the NAACP, which made Jon think there could be a problem, but that would not deter him from continuing with the project with or without their endorsement or commitment. Some people on the board were not his fans, but he hoped that they would not allow personal differences to determine support for a needed and worthwhile project. The Ivy Lane Project would benefit many children and their families, in the inner city. Regardless, the project would continue and would be successful, he would make sure of that.

Jon completed his meal and was not ready to go home just yet. He went to the PH to check out tea dance. This was the place to be on Sunday evening. He pulled into the parking lot and found a space. He checked himself to make sure he looked good, which he always did . He was a good-looking man. Wandering to the entrance of PH, he greeted the attendant and paid the cover. Once inside he started to dance on the disco lighted dance floor. He twirled, shimmied and swayed around. He had a great time at tea dance. He didn't close PH, he left around 11:00 p.m. Some alcohol. No coke. Some alcohol. No coke.

Jon finally made it home after the weekend with his parents.

He was exhausted, but in a good healthy way. His answering machine blinked to indicate that messages waited. He unpacked his bags and put his clothes away. He undressed and put on a pair of shorts and a t-shirt. He went to the living room and pressed his answering machine play button, the tape rewinded. He listened to the messages. Cyril left a message to tell Jon about his date with mister mister. Juan left several messages just to say hello, of course. Eric called to tell Jon, that he and Kelli are back together and he is considering changing professions. There was no message from an NAACP representative, but that was all right, also. Mel called just to say hello. Jon called Cyril.

"Hello," Cyril said.

"Hey, baby. What's up? Tell me all about mister mister. I know you can't wait to share all the sordid details. So, was mister mister all that you thought he would be?" Jon asked.

"Well, before I start to tell you about my weekend, how are the folks?"

"They are wonderful. Guess what else, they're in love! I mean, hand holding, giddy, school kids in love, in love. I was amazed. For the longest time I thought that my parents would eventually get a divorce and split up. This weekend, Cyril, they were a joy to watch. So much in love. I was just in awe of their glow. That's what I want, now. To have just a piece of that happiness."

"What do you mean in love? I thought your parents were always at odds with each other? What happened to make this phoenix rise from the ashes of their torrid marriage? I can say this because I'm their son," Cyril said.

"Some old man died from the church. He died alone and they wanted to die the same way. They decided to talk to each other instead of screaming and their love blossomed from their communicating. My mother even told me, she wishes I could find a man as good as my father. My mother told me to find a man. Can you believe that?"

"Mama said find a man? I can not can not believe that lie."

"You could have knocked me over with a boa. She never ceases to astonish me. She, no they told me that they just want me to be happy, however I can make it happen."

"Mama, she is a gem and I love her and your dad."

"They are quite special and I love them so much," Jon shared.

"As you should. I'm glad you went home for a visit. It has been awhile. Now, let me tell you about my weekend. Well, let me tell you, about me and Matt. I told you that were we going out Saturday night, right? So, Saturday afternoon, I home chilling out watching some old black & white movies I borrowed from the library. You, know a girl has to watch her coins. I was having a relaxing afternoon movies a couple of glasses of wine, some cheese. You know, being quite festive. Then the phone rang. It was Matt and I thought, oh, he is going to cancel. To my surprise not only did he not want to cancel, he wanted to check to see if we could get together earlier. That's a good sign, I thought."

"So, he came over and . . . ."

"At first I was skeptical, then I thought what would Jon do? I like you. Then I invited him over for a glass of wine before dinner. We had a wonderful afternoon talking about everything under the

sun. Jon, for the first time I was totally honest about everything. My hopes and dreams, fears and anguish. It was a great afternoon."

"Does it sound like you might have found him? Do you think he could be the one? Is he married, thing?"

"No, he is not married. Yes, he could be the one. From all indications we hit off very well. I am thankful that I have finally met a man for me."

"I am so glad that everything went so well with Matt. When will we get to meet mister Matt, anyway. I don't like it, when you go on dates with someone that I have not approved. So, give me the 411, what does he do, where is he from, who are his people and how old is he?" Jon teased.

"Where do I begin? First of all his is thirty with no children in the background. He has been out forever, that alleviates that problem. He is a public relations director for some publishing company here in town. So, he is all that I need and want, for now."

"What do you mean for now? I still need to make an appointment for you with a therapist don't I. He sounds like exactly what you need. Where is mister wonderful from?"

"Oh, he moved here from New York about a year ago to head the PR department at some publishing house. He doesn't get a chance to go out much, that's why we hadn't seen him out before. Thank God, the children would have eaten him alive if he'd been out more often. I'm glad he doesn't get out much."

"I'm glad too, because if he had been out more often you wouldn't have noticed because of mister Bruce, remember," Jon reminded him.

"Damn, you're right. Like I said, thank God he didn't get out much."

"Looks like I need to find a new party hound, because I know that you will be incognito after you two decide to become an item. Actually, maybe not. I might try to give up the party scene for a while and concentrate on me and the Ivy Lane Project. Who knows what might blow my way? Like I said, I hope he's a keeper."

"Me too. I have had enough married men, straight-gay men and all the rest of those types. I have found a gay man for once and I plan on keeping him and I hope he plans on keeping me, too?" Cyril said with reluctance.

"Stop, that doubting Thomas shit, he wants you just as much as you want him. So, you two will be an item, believe me. Now, do I have to ask again, when do I meet mister mister?"

Jon teased. "Well, let's get together tomorrow for happy hour, how does that sound?"

"That sounds like a plan, but ah, you have not told me about the rest of your evening with mr. wonderful. Do tell," Jon pressed.

"The rest of the night was magical. We planned an early evening since we got an early start. We had dinner, you guessed it, Bennigan's, but it was fun. We had a booth and talked and had a really good first date."

"What happened after Bennigan's? Where did you two end up? Your place, his place or . . .?"

"Well, since we took his car, we came back here so he could bring me home. He came in for a nightcap and . . .."

"You are not going to leave me there, are you?" Jon pleaded.

"We made out, we kissed and rubbed, but that's about it."

"Playing the innocent school girl routine. Nice touch."

"Now, Jon you know I am not like you. That is my normal first date, isn't it?" Cyril demanded.

"Yeah, boring. I wanted to hear something a little spicier. I guess I have to take what I can get. So, after you got each other hot and bothered then, what? Did he stay the night? Did he leave? What?"

"I wanted to ask him to spend the night, but I didn't know what he would think of me, as a prospective mate. That might make him think I'm some kinda slut. I didn't know, so I thought against it. That time I did not ask what would Jon do? I knew. You would have had the boy the same night and discarded him by Tuesday. I asked myself what would you do, but many times I do what I know is right for me, because I'm not you. I can't pull off some of your antics. I am not that talented yet. I'm working on it though," Cyril confessed.

"Don't. My life is not, as it appears to be. Keep doing the things that are right for you. They are the things are right for me too, but for a long time I didn't or did I want to know it. I have some issues to work out, that is one reason I went home this weekend. I needed to clear my head. Going home always, puts my mind at ease and I come back relaxed and ready for whatever life has to throw my direction."

"I'm glad you had a chance to rest and clear your head. You need to, with your big project coming up soon. Baby, I need to get off this horn, I got to hit early in the morning, I have an eight o' clock meeting. So, goodnight and I will call you tomorrow to make plans for you and Matt to meet. Talk at you later, bye."

"Sweet dreams talk at you, bye." Jon said and hung up the phone.

Jon was glad that he and Cyril had a chance to talk about their weekends and to express genuine love for each other. He was now on a mission to find a better place for some of his extra energy. The Ivy Lane Project would consume a great deal of his time, but he needed something more to fill the void that was on the horizon. Partying would not be high on the recommended list of activities, when he started therapy. Other diversions were needed. Tomorrow, he would take time to find other endeavors to occupy his free time. Taking a trip to New York would be the perfect excursion, before the project began, decided to call Juan make arrangements. It was late, but Jon called Juan anyway.

"Hello," Juan said in an up-beat Puerto Rican accent.

"Hey you," Jon said.

"Jon, how are you? I take it you got my messages?"

"Yeah, I did. Just calling to touch base and see when we can make some definite plans for me to visit. I have my day planner open and what's your schedule like in the next week or so?"

" . . . in the next week or so? I don't know if I can take the time off, on such short notice, but let me check with my supervisor and I will get back with you tomorrow. How does that sound?"

"That sounds great. Just call me with the info ASAP. So how are you? I haven't spoken with you in a couple of days. I apologize for the other night, I was coked out of my mind, as you probably guessed, since I never gave you an opportunity to speak, sorry."

"I didn't really know what was wrong so I called the next day and there was no answer, so I left a message. Are you okay? I was worried about you."

"No, I'm not really fine, but I'm coping. So, you were worried about me, were you?"

"Of course, I really do care about you, you know."

"I'm touched. I don't mean to make light of your feelings, lately I have been doing a little soul searching and my sentiment is sincere, not sarcastic. I am glad that you care about me, we can never have too many people care for us, now, can we?"

"What prompted you to do some soul searching, too much of the nasty and you worried about catching something . . . nasty? Just kidding."

"Actually nothing like that. I just am at a point in my life that I need more than what I have been receiving from . . . ."

"So, you want more than just sex. Is that it?"

"Well, yes I want . . .more. I need more. I deserve more. I will open myself up to have more. I'm sorry and I know this is horrible, even before, I say it. But I have met someone that I think could be the one, but the only problem is that he is involved in a relationship. If he wasn't in a relationship I know we could be magic together. I don't mean to diminish anything that we shared, but Ian just took me to another level. I can tell you this, right? Because first we decided to be friends who have sex when we get together, no strings, no commitments"

Juan was caught off guard with Jon's comments but did not allow it the hamper his conversation. He told Jon,"Right, right we are friends. So I'm glad that you feel that you can tell me about things that are happening in your life."

"Juan, I'm sorry for being so insensitive with your feelings. Sometimes I just don't think. I am so ... I don't ...caught up, raptured with my own shit that I forget about other people. Baby, I'm sorry. Can you forgive me?"

"Jon, of course. It's no big deal. We hit it a couple of times and hey it was great, but the bottom line you live in Florida and I live in New York. What was going to happen, it's not like I was transferring there or anything to be with you. We were not that deep," Juan said as he tore transfer paperwork and put it in the trash. Jon's new conquest ripped at Juan heart, but he could not allow Jon to know the truth, that he had touched him very deeply and that Juan wanted more from him.

"Juan, so when will you get back with me about my New York trip, I need some info as ASAP, okay? Juan, again I apologize for being insensitive. I will talk at you soon, bye babe."

"Cool Jon and take care of yourself, ciao," Juan said. Juan would not call Jon, again. The devastation Juan experienced from Jon's words wounded him emotionally although he would always have a warm spot in his heart for him. Jon never knew the emotional impact he had on Juan's life. He was so infatuated with Jon that he'd decided to transfer his job to be closer to him. Jon was not aware of the transfer or any other aspect of Juan's personal trauma, or would he ever.

Jon looked around the living room and was pleased that everything was clean and in place. He sat at his desk and contemplated his plight; how did he allow himself to sink to such depths of depression and loneliness, that his only solace was drugs and alcohol? He watched the warning signs, but did not stop to read them. For many many months the man–in–trouble signs were evident, but no one could see past Jon's brilliant disguise of the happy-go-lucky man. It was not difficult for Jon to deceive people when they thought that he was the man and he had everything under control.

He maintained a good job, with the help of a great assistant that kept the wolves at bay on days when he came to work late or not at all. He thought about the amount of alcohol he would consume a week and was repulsed. Jon thought a person of his caliber should not descend to the depths of depression and loneliness, to which he'd fallen. But that was the way with depression and loneliness; neither knew social, economic, racial or gender bias. He estimated the amount of money he'd spent on cocaine and the amount was staggering. He knew that he did not want a repeat of Thursday night.

In Jon's small town he enjoyed the simpler pleasures of family and the tranquility of sitting at the lake seeing the wonder of it all. He was able to commune with nature in way he could not in Orlando. He longed for the rocks at the lake, fields with soil as black as a million midnights that produced the best vegetables in the world. Living in a small town would be a fantastic outlet. Economically, he would not be able to find employment comparable to his position and salary in Orlando. He put thoughts of small town life out of his mind and looked toward the future in Orlando.

Jon was tired from the events of the day, his drive from home and partying at the PH. He went to his bedroom, undressed and took a quick shower to get the smoke out of his pores.

Deep in his spirit he knew that his life would be better, at any cost. He would do everything in his command to make his future the life he wanted to live, with or without that special someone to share in the joy and pain. He crawled into bed and drifted off to sleep with dreams and desires for a brighter tomorrow. The night enveloped him and he was at peace.

Monday, August 15, 1988

The morning sun swept across the city with force of a thousand suns. The city was awash with the radiance of golden illumination, glistening from the gleam the orb flung against the sky. The blinds were open and the sun shone through the room and gently caressed Jon awake. He awoke before his alarm clock blasted music.

He looked at himself in the mirror and was gladdened that he awoke alone, but was not lonely and as depressed as he had been in the past. He was determined to make the rest of the day a new adventure that would prove to be more exciting than the day before. He was on a quest to brighten each day more than the one before. Jon took a shower, dressed and was out the door; he'd grab a cup of java at the office.

Jon arrived at the office early for his work day. He greeted colleagues and staff members alike en route to his office. Claire had not arrived. He went in his office and pulled out his case files for the day. He had a full schedule and he intended to fulfill his duties as a therapist today at all cost. He reviewed the files and made some case notes on the progression of the clients and some therapeutic techniques he would employ today with each client. He even referred to some of his many journals on mental health counseling to detect methods of helping clients. Jon was on a new path and his perspective for his clients and himself was great. He saw the Jon he had not seen in a long time, the one that put his clients first. His clients always came first, but if he was coming to work under the hazy cloud of a Tanqueray induced hangover, he was not giving the clients his best. He had made a conscious decision to be the best therapist he knew how to be for his clients, because they deserved nothing but his best.

Claire poked her head into Jon's office and said, "Good morning. How are we doing this morning? I thought about you over the weekend, wondering if you were okay? How was your weekend?" "Claire, my weekend was fantastic. I had a wonderful time with my parents and I'm back in Orlando with a brand new perspective on my career, my personal life my . . . life. " I, to quote Patti LaBelle, have a new attitude". I will meet with Joel this evening to begin my new life of sobriety, not that my alcoholism had gotten out of hand, but I need to slow myself down,"

"Good, I'm glad you had a great weekend with your family. How are your parents doing anyway?"

"They are as giddy as schools kids. They are so much in love that it is sickening, but I am thrilled that they have found each other and are happy again."

"Well boss, let me get to work so I can justify my pay," Claire teased.

"You don't ever have to justify anything. You work hard for the money. I know you work with me and that's a job in itself."

"And on that note, I am at my desk," she said and took her seat behind her desk.

Jon returned to reviewing case studies in a journal when he remembered that he had not called his parents to let them know that he returned to Orlando safely. He had some time before his first client, so he picked up the receiver and dialed his parents' telephone number. The phone rang.

"Hello," Jon's mother said.

"Hey Ma, how are you?"

"Boy, you must have gotten lost? Why you just calling us to let us know you got home safe? I done told you time and again, call us so that we won't worry. We worry anyway, so don't give us extra reason to be concerned. Do I make myself clear, young man?"

"Yes Ma'am."

"I have heard that yes ma'am, before and you still don't call, but from now on, at least try."

"Mother, I am telling you from now on, I will be better. I just called to tell you that I love you guys and I'm glad you shared with me about your troubles and your reconciliation is that right, because you never really separated or anything?"

"Reconciliation is right. Although we never lived apart, we were separated for many years living in the same house sleeping in the same bed. We pray and thank God every night at how He has blessed us to find each other, again. Even though we were right there in each other's face for all those wasted years. Son, like we told you when you were with us over the weekend, don't let life pass you by. You got to get out and live."

"Ma, that's exactly what I plan to do. I am looking at my life from a totally different view and all I see if how bright my future is with or without someone to share it with. However, I am opening myself up to meeting new people and trying to trust. I have work to do on the relationship tip, but after what I saw you to share over the weekend, I think that anything is possible. I will keep my options open."

"Son, you know we love you and want only the best for you, so please be careful out there. Cuz, you know some of them children are crazy and I don't want nothing to happen to you."

"Ma, I am always careful. You and daddy taught me that a long time ago. I haven't forgotten all that I was taught. Ya'll raised me right and I am thankful for that. I have two wonderful parents that I love very much. Please relay that to Dad, too. Well I've got to get back to work, so I will talk with you later, love you."

"We love you too, baby. Call us soon. We miss you and we worry when we don't hear from you in a while. We don't like to call too much, you know, cramping your style, do the kids still, say that today? Well, we love you and don't be a stranger," she said and put the receiver on the cradle.

Jon returned to reviewing his case notes for his first appointment of the day. Mr. Mills, a man in his forties who needs a listening ear to help him cope with his compulsive behavior. He and Mr. Mills had made progress over the course of their relationship and Jon referred him to several psychiatrists, but Mr. Mills didn't want to continue his therapy with any of them. He thinks that only Jon can help him. He and Jon have worked through many of his problems, but had a long way to go. Mr. Mills arrived early for his appointment. He and Jon went into his office and started their session.

"Thank you Mr. Mills, I will see you at your next appointment, okay. Take care."

Mr. Mill did not respond. He simply continued about his path to the front door. Jon went back into his office and took out the case notes for his next client. He reviewed some more articles in his mental health journals. This was the Jon that prepared thoroughly for his session so as to be the best therapist he could

176

be. He liked the new Jon and he knew he would only get better for his clients. Jon had some time before his appointment and he decided to call Bella, Mrs. Tousaint and give her Nathan Anders' phone number, Nathan is a divorce attorney. He picked up the receiver and dialed her number, the phone rang. There was no answer he left a message,"Mrs. Toussaint, this is Jon I called to check on you and see how you were making out. Give me a call if you want talk, speak with you soon, bye."

"Jon, you have the African-American Philanthropic Foundation on line one."

"Thanks, Claire this could be the big one"

"I'll say a little prayer."

"This is Jon Knight, how may I help you?"

"This is Paige Johnson, with the African-American Philanthropic Foundation."

"This call to confirm that you received my grant proposal?"

"Well, yes we received your grant for funding assistance and we very impressed with the mission of the organization that you want to start. We think that more people need to give back to the community in ways other than writing a check, not that the checks aren't welcomed. However, your hands on approach outlined in your grant proposal is exactly the that type of program that we would like to see funded for the long haul. Your grant proposal had one other competitor for the funds. The grant proposal you presented edged out the competition. What made your proposal best suited for our foundation was the number of committed professionals willing to give of their time and efforts. The other factor was that you had corporations to commit, also."

"Wow, wait until I tell my assistant, she'll flip. When can I make a public announcement that the Ivy Lane Project will come to fruition?"

"We will mail official information and the budgetary constraints and all the guidelines that need to be adhered, to. By the end of the week everything on our end will be finalized and you can make an announcement next week."

"You have just made my week and it's only Monday. I don't know what I can do to thank you and the judging committee. I am so proud that the work of so many has come to a positive end, thank the powers that be."

"So, Mr. Knight keep us abreast of your announcement plans so that we can have representative present on that day. If you don't have any other questions I will let you get back to work and I will speak with you soon, take care."

Jon whirled around in his chair a few times before he stopped. He was ecstatic. Jon was so excited he did not know what to do next. The excitement was on so many levels that he did not know how to contain himself.

"Claire, get in here now!"

"What's wrong Jon?"

"What's wrong? What's wrong? Nothings wrong everything is right, everything is absolutely perfect. I need you to help put together a list of all the key media types in town!"

"For what purpose?"

"We need to set up a press conference for the announcement for not only the Ivy Lane Project, but for my proposal being selected as the model for projects across the country. Remember when I asked you to help me with the Ivy Lane Project and you were like, sure, not a problem. I didn't mention that I had applied for a grant to do the project on a national level locally for 18 months to work out the kinks and then on to key cities across the counrty."

"Wow, I am so excited for you. This is a wonderful opportunity and I'm just thrilled that everything has worked out so well for you." Her excitement was half-hearted because she knew that she would still be stuck at The Help Group, but she was gratful that Jon managed to get the time off to volunteer with the Ivy Lane Project.

"For me, what about you? Well I guess I need to tell you about the rest of the project. I want you to be my personal assistant, if you want the job. I know that you are loyal to the help group and all, but this could be an excellent oppotunity for you, and the kids. Now, the job will require some travel. Would you like to think it over for a few days and get back with me?"

"Let me see, a new position that will require some travel as your personal assistant. What is the salary and the benfit package?"

"Oh, I have taught you too well. Well your salary will in increase by 30% and your benefit package is much like The Help Group's, except we will offer a 401K plan and a 10% matching investment plan. So you have all the information, when should I expect a response?"

"Oh, I don't know? Give me a few minutes and I'll get right back to you. Well, I guess I will accept this new position! Thank you Jon for thinking of me."

"No, your loyalty to me, not necessarily to The Help Group, and your friendship is what I am thankful for. You have always had my best interests at heart, even when it seemed I didn't. You have saved my butt on numerous occasions and I don't forget freindship and loyalty. Besides where can I find an assistant as good as you are to me? I don't think that I can, so I better keep you around for as long as I can. I know you'll probably try to leave me, but I will be grateful for the years we've been a team. I do think of us as a team. Claire, thank you for all your hard work and dedication not only to this project, but to me personally."

"No, Jon thank you. You have always treated me like a valued assistant and not a servant and for that I am truly grateful."

"Okay, we need to get cracking on that media list for the press conference. I need to scout a location that might be suitable for the project offices. Hopefully we can hold the press conference at the new offices of the Ivy Lane Project. That name needs to change to be more cosmopolitan. I think we need a new name, any suggestions?"

"Call it The Project for Children, that's what its about right?"

"The Project for Children. I like it that will be the name of the national model, thanks Claire."

"Well, I need to get started on that media list. I'm at my desk if you need anything."

Jon and Claire had a very good working relationship which would only get better, now that Jon was working on his addictions. He would be the type of therapist and now executive director needed for this project. He was still walking on cloud nine. For Jon and Claire, the hardest part of their new found freedom was that they had to keep everything to themselves for the next week, but after that they could shout it to the world. He immediately started to prepare his invitation list for the reception that he needed to plan for the rest of the committee that helped with the grant and key community leaders, for public relations sake.

Jon thought how wonderful life was at this very moment and that he wished that he had someone to share it with, but he didn't. He started an inventory of his office in preparation of his departure in the next month or so. He didn't know how he would deal with Mr. Hamilton, but he would cross that bridge when the time was appropriate. Jon decided that he needed to share this with someone so he called his parents, but they were out. He decided to tell Cyril.

"Hello, this Cyril how may I help you."

"Hello, this is the executive director of The Project for Children."

"Jon, chile what are you talking about?"

"Remeber that grant proposal I was working on?"

"Yeah, how could I forget you only mentioned it about, oh a million times."

"Well, my proposal was accepted and this foundation is giving me the green light for my Ivy Lane Project and a national model program, budgeted for eighteen months."

"Wait a minute, what are you talking about? I thought that the program was for the Ivy Lane area?"

"Well, that's how it all got started, but while I was researching for the Ivy Lane project I found some grant information for a bigger project, so I submitted my proposal and there you have it. Thing, you cannot tell anyone, I mean anyone about this. I won't receive the official paperwork until next week. They gave me a verbal commitment over the phone, but was sworned to secrecy and here I am telling you."

"Jon, you know I can keep a secret. Congratulations my brother, I am so proud of you I could just spit. Well, when are we leaving The Help Group?"

"Probably not until the end of September, early October. I would need to conduct final interviews with clients and closing case notes and all that other BS. By the middle of October I should be in my new offices."

"I know you have already found your offices, haven't you?"

"Not exactly, but I need to be in the downtown area. Many of the people that I will have contracts with are in the downtown area, so that would work fine for me."

"We might have office space available in our buidling by then, would you like for me to check for you?"

"Yes, and I will check some other places, also. But, enough about me. How goes it with mister Matt? I hope that all is well and I'm looking forward to meeting him this evening. We are still on for drinks and dinner aren't we?"

"Of course. I want you and Matt to meet and become fast friends. I know that you will like him a great deal. Well, I will speak with you later I have an appointment and she's early. Later."

Jon put the receiver on the cradle. He was too excited to

work, but had a full schedule ahead of him today. He was on cloud eleven, his joy was too high for only nine. He whirled around in the chair and thought what should he do to celebrate his good fortune. He would treat himself to a wonderful lunch at *the cafe* and maybe a new everything for the press conference, shoes, suit,shirt, tie even underwear. His euphoria was overwhelming. Claire informed him that his next appointment had arrived. He greeted the client and proceeded with the session.

The early afternoon appointment cancelled, and Jon was free for the rest of the day. He left for a late lunch at *the cafe* and then to Winter Park for some shopping. He arrived at "the cafe" and pulled his car into the parking space. As he was parking he thought, *now I need a car more conducive to my new status*. He contemplated for a moment about cruising down Collins Avenue in Miami and was at his table for lunch. The smoldering aroma from the kitchen permeated his nostrils, as coke did, making his luncheon decision difficult. He looked over the menu and could not decide on his luncheon entree. Staring blankly at the menu waiting for something to jump from the page, he felt a tap on his shoulder. The sound of the tap on his shoulder awaken Jon from his menu coma.

"Are you having trouble deciding on a luncheon entree, sir?" he said.

Jon turned his head to see the person who tapped his shoulder, it was Ian. Jon was at a loss for words. Dumbfounded, Jon sat at his table and could not articulate a single syllable. What was happening? Was this the same man that made him feel, again? Was this Ian, whose letter word by word destroyed and rekindled his hope? Jon simply did not know what to do. He had not anticipated ever seeing Ian again, especially so soon after the letter. His emotions were raw, coursing through his veins. His heart oozed blood from being punctured by each comma, period and exclamation point of Ian's letter. Through the high emotional content of the situation Jon barely managed to find his voice and speak.

"Ian," Jon whispered.

"Hello, Jon," Ian said softly.

"I am just . . .," Jon did not complete his thought.

"Jon, I am sorry for the way it ended, what we never gave a chance to begin our passion. Since, then I have come to terms with myself and Enrique. I need to be there for him, but not stop living my life."

"How is . . . he?"

"Jon, I hope that you can forgive me for being a coward. What I felt for you made me question my love for Enrique and it frightened me. I was not supposed to be feeling those feelings for anyone except him. You brought a passion and fire that I had not experienced before and I was scared. So, instead of dealing with these desires, I extinguished them by cutting you out of the equation. Unfortunately, that did not work because I still think about you constantly. As I wrote in my letter my body ached for your touch and I could no longer endure not being with you, but I could not call you or come to see you, fearing that you would have nothing to do with me. When I saw you here today, my prayer was answered."

"I don't know what to say or do? I have spent the last week putting my life in order. Um, I . . . don't know quite what to say. When I read your letter I was devastated. We had spent the most glorious day, together. I knew that you had Enrique, but I. I don't know what I thought. I was so overwhelmed with these yearnings for you that I didn't give a damn about Enrique or anyone else, except you and me together. I know that may sound harsh but that is how I felt."

"You don't have to apologize. I understand what you're saying."

"Your letter crushed me. On the surface, to friends and family, I was fine with everything. Inside, I felt a gaping hole where my heart used to be. I would look in the mirror and lied to myself. I lied that I was fine. I would move on. Internally, I was void of hope."

"I know exactly what you mean. That's when I decided to talk with Enrique. We discussed our relationship. He was prepared for the conversation moreso that I was. He wanted to tell me to go and find someone new or at least meet so new friends, but was afraid of being alone. We had a very serious conversation, actually over the weekend. I will never leave him. He is really not well right now, but he insists on conducting life as normally as we can. So, we go out to lunch and dinner. Sometimes I think that we should take things little easier, but he won't have it any other way. His doctors only give him a few more months."

"I don't think, don't know if I could handle that, but if it was someone that I loved I would do all I could do to make their final days as peaceful as possible."

"I have tried to prepare myself for the inevitable. There is no way to prepare for the death of a loved one. He keeps telling that I will be all right, and I know in time the pain of his death will subside. This is just a painful situation. I have to live with him watching him slowly wither to death. I have tried to keep my spirits up, but it's hard."

"I know death is a difficult transition and in many cases the difficulty is for the living. The living have to continue on after the loved one has passed. Grieving is a process that you will take you through everything from denial to finally accepting that a loved on is really gone."

"That's where I was, preparing for the worst and then, on top of all that drama, I meet you. My whole world was turned upside down and I didn't know what to do?"

"Well, what did you and Enrique decide about you and your future?"

"Like I told him I will not leave him. I need to be with you, but I don't want to be with you like this, I want you to have all of me. As, long as Enrique is alive I can't be with you completely. I don't want you to be the other man. It's not fair to you, me or Enrique. I want you, but not at this point in my life. Like I wrote, timing is a bitch. Have you seen that old movie from the fifties, *An Affair to Remember*?"

"Yeah, sure. Is that where this is going? We make a date, for what, six months from today to meet here for lunch?"

"No, more like a year. That will have given me time to grieve and be ready for another relationship, maybe. Who knows what the future holds. I know that I could easily fall in love with you. Unfortunately, the time is not right. I pray that the intensity for each other never wavers. Jon it has been wonderful seeing you again. I wish I could stay and talk, but Enrique is about done with his chemotherapy and I want to be there when he's finished. Jon, take care of yourself, and I love you and I will see you in one year, if you are still available."

"Nothing could keep me from it. I love you, too. I'll see you next year. Same bat time same bat station."

Ian and Jon embraced. They said their good byes and Ian was gone. Jon was in shock. Seeing Ian made Jon want him even more. He watched as Ian got in his car and drove away. That would be the last time Jon would see Ian. A tear trickled from Jon's eye. He wiped it away and would not allow any more to be released.

Jon had closure, now he could move on with the knowledge that this one true love was gone. He had held Ian for the last time. His mind, a blank canvas waited for images of his life without Ian to take form. He envisioned himself in a relationship, happy. Unfortunately, the relationship would be without the intense passion he'd shared with Ian. Jon was at peace.

Sitting in "the cafe", Jon still had not decided what he wanted for lunch, so he ordered the special, shrimp scampi. A sparkling glass of white zinfandel sat in front of Jon, he gazed into the liquid and was lost in his thoughts of lost love. He picked up the glass and white zinfandel surged through his body, making him lucid more animated than normal.

He finished his lunch and decided that he would not return to the office. He called his office and told Claire that would see her the next morning, early. Jon got in his car and drove. Jon had solace and a firm grasp of his emotions. Today was one of the best days of his life and he was determined not to allow regret to ruin it.

The black mustang ended up on the shores of the Atlantic ocean. Jon got out of the car and walked along the beach. He was communing with nature. Leaving his shoes in the car he rolled up his pants and walked in the water. The water soothed him in a way that he had not felt for a long time. The more he walked, the better he felt about his outlook. He needed to feel the way he did early in the day, before he talked with Ian. He was ready for a new and challenging career move. Opening his heart and mind, not allowing disappointment to hinder his pursuit of happiness with someone new, was his mission.

Making it just in time for his six o'clock appointment Jon walked into Joel's office to begin his first session. Being on a therapist's couch for help was a new experience for Jon, one that would prove helpful. Deciding not to take the couch for his first session, Jon sat across from Joel, ready for the seesion to start.

"Mr. Knight what made you come to therapy?" Joel asked Jon.

This is the same question Jon had asked clients a million times, but it was the first time it had been directed to him. Squirming in his seat like a child with his hand caught in the cookie jar, he responded to Joel.

"Damn that's a hard question. Joel, you know I never realized how difficult it was to sit on the other side of the therapy chair. Questions, like that make you probe you innerself to find real answers to the perplexing questions" Jon responded.

"Yes, you are right, the questions make you probe yourself to find the answers. Mr. Knightwhat made you come to therapy?"

"I just need someone to talk with that can understand me."

"Mr. Knight, I'm sure that you have friends that you can talk with. If that's all you needed then I am sorry I wasted your time tonight. Make an appointment with me when you can answer the first question."

"Joel, come on let's talk. Waking up with dried blood on my face and body, lying in my trashed apartment, made me come to therapy. There is that a good enough answer for you?"

"Only if it is the truth. Progress can only be made if you work with me to help you find the answers to questions that you have. Answering the tough questions will make therapy a breeze and you will be in and out in nothing flat, but if you don't cooperate then sessions are futile."

"Depression and sexual addiction, that's why I came to therapy."

"That is what you are experiencing, but what made you come to therapy? That is the question on the table, Mr. Knight."

Sitting there not sure what the right answer was for Joel, but knowing the truth. Therapy would help much more than Jon imagined. He assumed since he was a therapist and he knew his diagnoisis that therapy would be a piece of cake, he was mistaken. Sensing that therapy would probe deeper into his psyche than he thought, Jon was beginning to think that therapy was a huge error in judgment. Therapy would make Jon face some ugly realities in his past that were buried deep in the abyss that was his soul of souls. Pangs of anxiety washed over Jon and he was overwhelmed with fear that someone would see him naked, bare of all secrets. Exposure to the real Jon was rare, only a few people ever experienced that phenomenon. Therapy would lift the cloak of secrecy from around the guarded wall Jon lived behind.

Answering the questions would open the floodgates to the real Jon. He was afraid to know what lurked in the darkness. Fear that the real Jon was the one that really enjoyed being high and drunk and fucking without condoms. Maybe the real Jon was the Notorious Knight, after all. Revealing Jon would settle many questions that had been pushed out of his consciousness and into the vacuous ocean of his idle mind. Resting on his ass, Jon looked at Joel and the first brick was removed. A single tear escaped his eye and he quickly wiped it away.

"Okay, I feel that there is more to life than what I'm getting and I want to figure out what is it that I'm not doing it right? I am a successful therapist with a great career, but I can't seem to get it together. I came to therapy because I need to find answers to questions I've been asking myself for a long time. Why do I use cocaine, I know the damage that it can cause, but I still sniffed?"

He paused and held his head in his hands. He looked up and more bricks fell. The wall was about to come tumbling down. Sitting there in the therapist's clients chair, he tried to keep the tears from flowing, but he couldn't. A long while passed while Jon composed himself and prepared to continue his first session.

"What was I avoiding hiding in the Tanqeray bottle? How did I allow myself to slip so far into this depression that my only solace was coke, liquor and . . . sex? The more sex I had, the better I felt about myself and the more powerful I felt."

"Okay, now were getting somewhere. What is it that you think you aren't getting from life?

"Love."

"Love?"

"Yes, love. I have had numerous sex partners and a good number of relationships, but never have I felt love with any of these people. Recently, I met someone that I connected with, I think that I could have fallen in love with him, but I don't know,"

"What happened with him?"

"Well the long and short of it was that he cheated on his lover, who is dying of AIDS complications, with me. There was such a geniune affection for each other. We were just in awe of each other in the respect that we felt something real between us. We only had one day together, but that day changed me."

"Changed you, how?"

"He made me feel. I liked it and I want that, again. "

"Haven't you felt that before? Have you been in love before?"

"Yes, I have been in love, but the passion that I felt with Ian was immeasurable. What I felt with him was incredible." .

"Why do you think you felt such intensity with him?"

"Because with him I was totally myself. I felt that I needed to let the real me surface and when I did we had a chemistry that was devastatingly special. He saw me naked, like in the biography about Josephine Baker, *Naked at the Feast*, and I was just me."

"So, being just you, how is that different from how you are other times?"

"I say what I really mean and not try to give glib or sly answers. When I am not trying to be, when I just am."

"Jon, I think that you have most of the answers to your questions, why are you really here? There is nothing I can ask you that you haven't asked yourself already. What is it that you need? You know the answers to your drug questions. How have you decided to handle your sexual addiction?"

"I put myself on a self- imposed sexual hiatus. I do this periodically. Because I need time to focus on my other issues and that didn't seem to be as pressing as the others."

"Like I asked you before, why are you here, Jon? Do you want someone to monitor you, someone that you have to report to? I am not understanding, what is it that you need?"

"I want to be drug-free. I don't know if I can do it alone. The weekend was a struggle, but I was home with my parents so that made it easier. What happens when I am here in Orlando around some of the people that I did cocaine with, what happens then?"

"What happens then is that you will have to make a decision. Do I use or not? Only one person can make that choice for you and this is you and nobody else."

"I know, I am the only one that can decide whether or not to sniff cocaine or not. I have put a stop to it so far, but I don't know about the tomorrows?"

"You have to take it one day at a time or if that's too long break it down further, to mornings. If you have to take one hour at a time, but since you went the entire weekend I don't forsee any problem with taking it one day at a time."

"You are right, Joel I think I just needed to sit with a respected colleague to help me come to the realizations I already knew. Thereapy makes it all seem real that I have issues and I need to work through them, although I have made choices about most of them already. Do you have any input to my form of treatment?"

"As far as I'm concerned you never needed a session, but I am pleased that you thought enough of my expertise to make an appointment with me. Thanks for the confidence."

"I've respected your judgment with many clients. I have reviewed your case notes before and agreed with your treatment plans nine times out of ten. When I didn't agree it was just a personal choice of treatment."

"Fine, I have about the same ratio when I've reviewed you case notes. So, do you want to make another appointment for about three months from now? However, if for any reason you need to talk call me or we can meet, whenever you need."

"In three months, sounds good and I will keep you abreast of my progress," Jon agreed.

"I'll will talk with you tomorrow."

"I'll will see you in the a.m."

Fresh from his first therapy session Jon looked around the restaurant for Cyril and Matt. He spotted them sitting at a table by the window overlooking the Lake Eola. White linen table clothes, glowed from the flicker of candle light in the main dining room. Jon joined Matt and Cyril at the table by the window. Cyril and Matt were enjoying a glass of wine. Jon decided to have cola instead.

"So, this must be Matt, hello I'm . . ." Jon said before he was interrupted by Matt.

"Jon, I presume," Matt said.

"Correct and you must be Matt? Very nice to meet you."

"Likewise I'm sure," Matt said offering his hand.

"You done good.   He's attractive, pleaseant and mannered, he stood to shake my hand.   I like him," Jon directed his comment to Cyril.

"Don't mind him. He just likes to act like my big brother, even though we are the same age. Him and his parents are the closest to family that I have. So, prepare for the interrogation, which will ensue, believe me." Cyril said to Matt.

"Stop that Cyril, you're gonna make him think that I'm some kinda ogre. I just want to make sure that he is good enough for my little brother.   Our parents aren't here to the honors, so that leaves the dirty work to me."

"Cyril is very fortunate to have a friend, someone that genuinely cares about him the way that you do. He has told me so much about you, I feel like I know you already. I am ready to answer any questions that you might have about me, my family, my job, how I feel about Cy, anything."

"That's enough. Our dinner's here. If I feel the need to interject a small inquiry, I might," Jon said.

"He will ask and I know he has a list of questions that he will get to while we're eating dinner," Cyril said.

"Jon, let me give you a brief history about me and if I leave anything out, please don't hesitate to ask for clarity," Matt said.

"I'm all ears," Jon said.

"I was born and raised in Savannah, with two older brothers and two younger sisters, I'm right in the middle. I went to Beach High School and Savannah State College. I've been gay all my life. A praticing homosexual since I was nineteen, and I'm thirty now. I have had two significant relationships, both ended badly. Well I shouldn't say badly, they were not ready for a serious relationship. I've been in Orlando for about a year and I don't get out too much, my job is very demanding and I travel a great deal. I moved to Orlando from New York."

"You moved from New York to Orlando? Let me check your temperature. Why on earth would anyone move from New York to Orlando?" Jon asked.

"An opportunity of a lifetime. I was offered a position to head the public relations department for a major publishing house. The opportunity was too great for me to turn down, besides the benefits and other perks that came with the offer. To add icing to the cake, I've gone and met Cy, who is going to be with me for the long haul I hope and pray?"

"Matt you have said all the right things and I hope that you are all that you appear to be. If you are not I will hunt you down like a dog! Please be all that you say you are," Jon said.

"Okay enough Jon, let's enjoy our dinner. You know enough about Matt and he is all that he appears to be." Cyril said.

"Jon I am glad that Cy has a friend like you in his corner. I hope that you will always be there for him . . . and us?"

Dinner was a huge success Jon thoroughly enjoyed meeting Matt and spending the evening with him and Cyril. Cognac and coffee was how they ended the evening. Jon gave Matt and Cyril a big hug and was on his way home. He would not drop by the PH tonight too see what was hanging out, he would go straight home.

Relaxing at his desk Jon thought about his day, which was great. Today was a day of new beginnings and happy and bittersweet endings, he thought of Ian and a year from today. Who knew what the future held in store, but he was not about to wallow in disappointment. His life was going through too many fantastic changes to let anything or anyone get him down. Professionally, Jon was at the top of his game and nothing would stand in his way of being the best at his new position. Heading the Ivy Lane Project that would become the national model for programs around the country was the best thing that had happened to Jon in his entire life. His proposal was powerful, but he had no idea that it would catapult him to national prominence for his work with children. Having the support of the local chapters of national organizations helped locally and he hoped would help secure the support on a national level. Jon Knight's life was on the rise and his future looked brighter than he'd ever imagined.

Cyril would no longer have to settle or accept less than he deserved. Knowing his brother, dear Cyril, had found someone special, pleased Jon. He was a good person with a kind heart. Unfortunately, his family did not and would never see that side of him, because of their prejudice and issues with his homosexuality. Cyril, for the first time, was ready and willing to be with a man who was decidedly gay and he would not have to settle for limited time with his new lover. Cyril was embarking on a love affair that Jon wished would last forever.

Jon thought about, Bella Toussaint, his client and friend. She had become, although he didn't know her that well or had he known her long, important to Jon. Knowing her situation made Jon glad she'd come through her trials with Bruce and was moving on. She planned to return to school and become a mental health counselor, she wanted to help other women that might be in or have been in her situation. She now realized that she was not alone in her plight and she would continue to meet with

Jon, monthly. Jon and Bella would move from sessions to dinners, not client and therapist, but friends having dinner.

Stars spangled against the midnight blue sky caressed the city, with the intensity of a passionate lover. Standing on his terrance, Jon saw a falling star and made a wish. He whispered his wish to the night, "I wish my life and the lives of all in my life, will progress at the pace that is needed for each of us." He went inside closing the door behind him. In his bedroom Jon did something that he had not done in a very long time, he prayed. Jon crawled into bed alone, which was the way he wanted it, and his slumber was uninterrupted.

Tuesday, August 16, 1988

The city was still asleep when Jon was awaken by the gentle stroke of the sun, as the rays washed across his bedroom and illuminated his face. Warm sun rays welcomed Jon into a new day. He was glad that the creator had spared him one more day.

Jon was at peace with all aspects of his life. All the pieces of Jon's life had fallen into place. He was about to embark on the adventure of a lifetime as the executive director of the Project for Children. Turning to the next page of his life, Jon knew that today would be the beginning of a new start. On his terrace, he looked over the city and was thankful for all that he had and regretted nothing. He stood in awe and respected the presence of the creator in all that he saw.

Today was the first day of the rest of Jon's life and he was doing what he needed to do with it. Living, sharing and for once in his life, Jon was making an effort to love himself, if no one else. His new mantra he'd adopted was, "Lord, help me not abuse cocaine, alcohol or most importantly my body, today." Jon "Notorious" Knight was no longer detached

If you would like to order this or any other Ishai Book or a catalog, copy and fax or mail to:

Ishai Books
The Ishai Creative Group, Inc.
709 East Caracas Street
Tampa, Florida 33603-2328
813/234.6410 • Fax: 813/236.8809
E-Mail: IshaiBooks@aol.com

Name: _____

Store/Company: _____

Address: _____

City, State: _____ Zip: _____

Phone: (_____)_____ Fax: (_____)_____

Ordered by: _____

Ship to: _____

(If different) _____

Quantity	Description	Cost	Unit	Total
	Like Breathing • 1-892096-33-1 **Ricc Rollins** Retail: $14.00			
	Colorblind • 0-9669271-0-9 **Judy Candis** Retail $12.00			
	Detached • 1-892096-35-8 **Lorenzo C. Robertson** Ret. $14.00			
	The Best Man • 1-892096-01-3 **Dwayne Carter** Retail $ 14.00			

Sub-total	
S/H	$3.95
Total	

Method of Payment:

◯Cash ◯ Check #:_____ ◯Visa•MC•AMEX ◯C.O.D

• Minimums Apply•

Please Make Checks Payable to The Ishai Creative Group, Inc.